Whispers of Treason

An Ed Maddux novel

ALSO BY R.J. PATTERSON

Ed Maddux series
King of Queens
To Catch a Spy
Whispers of Treason

Cal Murphy series
Dead Shot
Dead Line
Better off Dead
Dead in the Water
Dead Man's Curve
Dead and Gone
Dead Wrong
Dead Man's Land
Dead Drop
Dead to Rights
Dead End

James Flynn series
The Warren Omissions
Imminent Threat
The Cooper Affair
Seeds of War

Brady Hawk series
First Strike
Deep Cover
Point of Impact
Full Blast
Target Zero
Fury
State of Play
Siege
Seek and Destroy
Into the Shadows

Whispers of Treason

An Ed Maddux novel

R.J. PATTERSON

FIRST EDITION

Cover art by Dan Pitts.

The evil that men do lives after them;
The good is oft interred with their bones.

— WILLIAM SHAKESPEARE

APRIL 1965, BELGRADE, YUGOSLAVAKIA

JOVAN DIVAC JAMMED his hands into his pockets and felt the pair of envelopes he had been handed. One was full of cash. The other? He wasn't sure what comprised its contents, but he wasn't going to look or ask either. The less he knew, the better. The mere act of carrying such a package put him at risk if he happened to get caught by the SDB, Yugoslavia's secret police. But given the employment opportunities in Belgrade—or lack thereof—Divac didn't hesitate to take such a gamble. With a wife and two young daughters to take care of, he couldn't refuse paying work, even if it was dangerous.

Divac spent the next hour circling a lengthy path of more than a dozen city blocks. On days when his handyman work was nonexistent, his routine consisted of stopping regularly at random cafes to kill time as well as avoid suspicion from any SDB agents milling around. They were always watching.

He ducked into a coffee shop and ordered a cup of coffee. When he went to pay, he looked down and realized he'd grabbed a one thousand dinar note from his envelope. Divac was sure he'd arranged them in a manner so he wouldn't draw a wary look from any store owners who love to earn a handsome tip for turning in someone behaving suspiciously.

"Do you have anything smaller?" the man asked as he shook the bill.

Divac chuckled and shook his head before handing over ten dinar note. "I wouldn't want to exchange my monthly rent payment for a cup of coffee, would I?"

The man snatched the cash from Divac and then handed him his change. Divac took a deep breath then drank his coffee slowly, glancing at the man periodically.

One of Divac's neighbors, Drajan Kovac, settled into a chair across from Divac. Kovac leaned forward, hunching over his coffee. He glanced around the room before speaking in a hushed tone.

"They're everywhere, you know," Kovac said.

"Who?" Divac asked.

"The SDB, that's who. Even when you think they aren't watching you, they are."

Divac shook his head. "If you're that convinced the SDB is everywhere, should you be speaking with me like this in public?"

"You're probably right." Kovac stood up suddenly and moved to an empty seat across the room.

After five minutes, Divac turned to see the store owner casting a wicked glare. Divac froze and tried to act natural. But the man kept his gaze trained on Divac all while yanking the phone off the hook and dialing a number. Divac took another sip and tried to read the man's lips. As soon as Divac realized the man had mouthed for someone to get to his shop immediately, Divac bolted for the door.

Hustling down the street, Divac searched for a way to blend in even as the store owner followed behind. He shouted to a pair of SDB agents on the opposite sidewalk and pointed at Divac.

Divac kept his head down as he wove in and out of the pedestrian traffic, keeping track of the men pursuing him with shifty glimpses of the scene behind him. The agents pursued him in silence, which Divac used to his advantage. Had he been a thief, the Belgrade police would be begging the public to stop him, but the SDB preferred to remain low key. Despite their attempts to be almost invisible through low-profile activities, the residents of Belgrade could spot SDB personnel from several blocks away. Everyone had either been the recipient of an SDB visit or watched as agents corralled a suspect to the ground. And their pristine suits made them stand out in crowds, especially in a district full of mostly skilled laborers.

Divac used the trick his CIA contact had shared once the job began. Confidently, Divac turned the corner and disappeared down an alleyway, using the clothes hung across lines to obstruct the agents' views. He dashed out the other side and across the street, meandering along another route until he lost them.

That was easy.

He looked up and was face to face with an SDB agent.

"We need to talk," the agent said.

Divac's instinct was to run, but the gun trained on him convinced him otherwise. He raised his hands slowly.

"What is this all about?" Divac asked.

9

"This way," the agent said, using his weapon to direct Divac.

He walked cautiously in front of the agent, meandering through several alleyways until they reached a furniture store. Once inside, they went to the back of the store and entered a door that opened up into a small windowless room. Fluorescent lights hummed overhead in what was an otherwise eerily quiet space.

"Did I do something wrong?" Divac asked as he sat down.

The agent eyed Divac carefully. "You tell me."

Divac looked down. "I do everything that is asked of me. I am loyal to this country."

The agent nodded. "That is why we came to you. We've been looking for you for a while."

The other agent stepped forward. "We believe your neighbor is a spy."

"Mrs. Cacic? The old lady with the poodle?" Divac asked.

"Looks can be deceiving. We have recorded a series of coded messages she tried to pass to a man that we believe is an American spy." The agent slid a picture across the table to Divac. "You have probably seen this man in your apartment."

Divac swallowed hard and nodded. The picture he was staring at was also his contact.

"If you know this man is a spy, why not eliminate him now?" Divac asked.

"That is not how the SDB operates," the agent said. "We must be sure that all strands of the web are severed before we go after the primary target."

"So, how can I help?"

"It is a simple request. We want you to slide her a message underneath her door while she is out walking her dog. We need to confirm that this is how the spy is communicating with her."

"That's all?"

The agent nodded. "Do you think you can do that for us?"

Divac exhaled slowly and slid his fingers along the envelope tucked inside his jacket. "It would be my honor to help the SDB in this way."

He stood and pushed the chair back with his knees before collecting the document.

"We will be watching," the agent said. "You can show yourself out."

Divac wound his way through the store before emerging onto the sidewalk. Despite agreeing to help the SDB, Divac wasn't sure if he wanted to.

Perhaps this is a trap and they're testing my loyalty.

Divac considered that possibility and many others as he walked home for lunch.

While contemplating his next move, Divac ascended the steps leading to his apartment. He plodded upward while his eyes were cast downward, his own footsteps echoing in the stairwell. But a different noise made him stop and look up.

Mrs. Cacic was standing on the landing ahead of him, clutching her poodle. Their eyes locked, increasing Divac's angst.

Was she really a spy for the Americans too? Or was she a spy for the SDB being used to ferret out his loyalties?

His mind raced, unable to settle on the likeliest outcome.

"Good day, Mr. Divac," she said, nodding politely as she passed him.

"Good day, Mrs. Cacic."

Divac wanted to slide the envelope underneath her door and be finished with his task. If she was spying for the Americans, he had almost decided she would have to deal with the fallout herself. He lingered at the top of the steps, watching her descend and disappear from sight before making another move. After she was gone, he shoved his hand in his pockets and reached for the message. Instead, he felt the package of cash, causing him to ponder his own situation.

Would I want someone else to be so cavalier about my life?

Divac held the envelope up to the light but couldn't read anything. He clearly saw something written on the paper, helping him reach the conclusion that it wasn't a dummy note. But such information didn't enable him to rule out anything. A blank note would've only proven that the task was about deciphering where his loyalties rested. But an actual note? The stakes were officially raised. He needed to see what was written inside.

Divac entered his apartment to find his wife and two young daughters playing in the living room. The two girls ran up to greet him, each clinging to one of his legs. He tousled their hair and knelt before kissing them both. His wife, Maja, stood a few feet away, waiting her turn to kiss her husband.

Divac peeled the girls off his legs before turning his attention to Maja. They locked lips briefly before Divac withdrew as he knit his brow.

"What is it?" she asked.

"That smell," he said. "Are you making my favorite?"

She smiled and nodded. "Chicken soup."

"But it's not even Sunday. You never make that on any other day of the week."

"I thought you deserved a good surprise with how stressful work has been for you lately."

He flashed a faint smile.

"Thank you," he said as he eyed the boiling pot in the kitchen.

"Are you ready to eat now?"

"I need to put a few things away. Maybe in five minutes."

"Okay," she said before returning her attention to the girls, who were tugging on her dress.

Divac eased into the kitchen and glanced over his shoulder to make sure Maja wasn't watching. He pulled out the note from the SDB agent and held it over the steam. Divac nervously looked back in the living room at his wife, hoping she hadn't noticed.

Come on, come on.

The adhesive had started to loosen up but not enough that he could open the letter without giving away the fact that it had been resealed.

"Putting away some things?" Maja said from the living room. "It looks like to me you are inhaling the fumes from the chicken soup."

Divac held the letter close against his chest and looked over his shoulder at Maja. "Am I not allowed to enjoy the aroma of my beautiful wife's delicious cooking?"

She smiled and shook her head. "I know what you are doing. But I thought you knew by now that I do not respond to flattery. Despite your best efforts, I will not be making chicken soup every day for you."

"A man can dream."

He watched her engage with the girls again, tickling the youngest, Sasha, which resulted in a lengthy episode of non-stop giggling. Refocusing on his task, Divac eased the envelope back over the steam and waited a few more seconds. He slid his finger along the flap, which separated easily. He retreated back to his room, checking to make sure all the blinds were pulled before reading the message.

After he shut the door, Divac dropped to his knees and opened the letter. Scrawled inside was a short directive: "Kill him tonight, and make sure other tenants know about it."

Kill who tonight?

Divac's paranoia convinced him that he was Mrs. Cacic's target, even though the idea sounded preposterous—a seventy-five year-old assassin. But no one else lived in her apartment, so it had to be her. Divac considered for a moment the possibility that she was merely a courier herself and would be delivering that message to someone else, but he dismissed the idea almost as soon as it entered his mind.

Mrs. Cacic is an assassin, not for the Americans but for the SDB.

Heaviness settled over Divac. He had to deliver the message now. If Mrs. Cacic didn't get the note, the SDB would come after him. Yugoslavia's secret police were testing his allegiances. If she did get the note, he could be the target and might end up dead. Both scenarios were unacceptable to him, though the latter sounded somewhat preferable. At least if he was prepared, he would have a chance against an elderly woman, depending on her method of delivery.

He loosened one of the floorboards beneath his side of the bed and stashed away the money he'd received from his CIA contact. He was pressing the board back into place when Maja entered the room.

"Jovan, is everything all right?" she asked, her brow furrowing. "What are you doing down there?"

"Just tidying up," he said as he scrambled to his feet.

"Are you sure everything is okay? You seem distracted today."

He kissed her on the cheek. "Everything is fine. Let's go eat some chicken soup."

Over lunch, they discussed the general happenings at home and at work. As usual, Divac lied, making up a story about one of his favorite fictional customers. While he worked as a messenger for the CIA, his wife believed his handyman business was his only source of income. In reality, he rarely did any work for anyone else.

"How does a man who acts like that survive in this world?" Maja asked, which was the same question she wondered aloud after every such story her husband told about a disagreeable client.

"It's all about *who* you know," he said, "not *how* you act."

"Guess he knows someone important then," she said, completing the repeated conversation.

He stood. "I have to get going now," he announced before stooping down next to Maja and kissing her. He kissed both his daughters on top of their heads and then hustled back to his bedroom. Digging the message out of his pocket, he resealed the envelope and hid it by draping his jacket over his arm. Once he exited his apartment, he slipped up to Mrs. Cacic's door and slid the note underneath.

He heard footsteps down the hall and immediately stood upright, spun on his heels, and strode toward the stairwell. Looking up, he noticed Mrs. Cacic returning from her walk with her poodle.

* * *

LATER THAT EVENING, Divac returned home with a plan to keep Mrs. Cacic at bay. Subtlety was vital. He walked into the kitchen after getting mobbed by his girls and Maja.

"Do we have any more of that chicken soup left?" he asked.

Maja arched her eyebrows. "I know you like that soup, but I didn't know you would prefer to eat it several times a day."

"Actually, I wanted to take a bowl over to Mrs. Cacic," Divac said. "I saw her on the sidewalk this afternoon after lunch and she looked sad. She told me it was the anniversary of her husband's death from seven years ago."

"*Dušo*," she said. "You are too sweet. Let me heat it up and ladle a bowl for you."

"I appreciate it," Divac said. "I'm going to go change."

In his bedroom, Divac changed into some more casual clothes and then rushed to open the plank in the floor where he kept his cash. A small vial given to him by his CIA contact was also nestled beneath the stash of money. Holding the poison up to the light, Divac didn't notice much inside. He had never even checked it, hoping that he would never have to use it.

"One drop for someone else if you want it to be discreet and appear like a heart attack," the agent had said. "Two drops or more if you want a quick way out or you need someone to die almost immediately."

Just one drop for you, Mrs. Cacic.

Divac pocketed the poison and re-covered his hiding place. Easing back into the kitchen, he saw Maja standing over the counter while preparing a bowl of soup on a tray.

"One steaming hot bowl of chicken soup for Mrs. Cacic," she said as she handed the food to Divac. "Tell her that I am thinking of her."

"Of course," Divac said before taking the tray.

Maja opened the door for Divac. "I can come with you," she said. "And the girls, too."

"No, no," he protested. "It'll only take a minute, less time than it would for you to round everyone up."

"Fine," she huffed. "Just don't stay gone long. I want to talk with you about something."

"Okay," Divac said as he exited their apartment.

He steadied the tray as he strode down the hallway. Stopping a few feet short of Mrs. Cacic's door, he pulled the vial out of his pocket and tapped out one drop of poison. He mixed it in using the spoon and proceeded to knock on the door.

"Why, Mr. Divac," she said without a hint of a smile, "you shouldn't have."

"I care about you, Mrs. Cacic. I thought you might enjoy a bowl of hot soup tonight, maybe keep you off your feet a bit."

"I actually love to cook," she said as she took the

bowl. "Come inside if you wish. I know you're not just here to deliver me a meal."

Divac didn't move.

She motioned for him to come in. "Come on, now. No need to be stubborn about this."

Mrs. Cacic turned her back on Divac and hobbled inside. For a moment, he considered turning around and leaving, but he doubted she would eat the soup if he did. But he followed her lead, leaving the door wide open as a matter of safety.

"What's wrong with you?" Mrs. Cacic asked as she turned and noticed the door open. "I cannot heat all of Belgrade."

Divac hustled back and pushed the door almost shut, leaving it cracked just a smidge. When he turned back around, Mrs. Cacic was shuffling toward the kitchen.

"Did you hear about Drajan Kovac?" she asked as she sat down at the table.

"The plumber in 4C?"

She nodded. "He's the one—and he's dead."

"Dead? What happened to him?"

"If anyone knows, they aren't saying. It only happened a few hours ago."

"How did you—"

"I passed by his unit as they were wheeling him out into the hallway. The doctor helping said it appeared to be a heart attack. But you never know for sure, do you?"

"You think someone did this to him?" Divac asked, his suspicion of her reaching an all-time high. He would bet his life on the elderly woman being an assassin for the SDB.

She shrugged. "Maybe. But that doesn't really matter now. He's gone, and I've got no one to fix my pipes that burst last night. Think you might be able to help me? I know you're a handyman. It would surely be more helpful than bringing me a bowl of this soup."

Divac watched as Mrs. Cacic brought the spoon up to her mouth and stopped short before setting down her utensil. He was barely paying attention enough to answer her question, thinking hard about what she had said before responding. But he never received an opportunity to retort as she continued her thought.

"You know, I wish we had more men like Mr. Kovac around. He never even charged me for all the work he did for me. Guess he had plenty of money, though I have no idea where it came from. One of a kind that man, I tell you." She gestured toward the seat across from him. "Please, have a seat."

He pulled out the chair across from her and settled into the seat.

"Tell me about your day," she said. "Did your work go well?"

Divac eyed her closely, trying to sort out everything clattering around in his head. For starters there was the anticipation of Mrs. Cacic actually slurping down a spoonful of the soup. There was also her tone, one that made Divac uncomfortable.

Is she doing this on purpose? Does she know the truth about me?

There was an even bigger question nagging Divac. *Did she kill Mr. Kovac?*

Before he could answer, a knock at the door interrupted their conversation.

"Would you mind getting that? My feet are a little sore this evening," Mrs. Cacic said.

Divac nodded and strode toward the door, opening it to find his wife.

"Maja, what are you—"

"I thought I would come check on Mrs. Cacic, too."

Divac looked down and noticed his two daughters in tow.

"Come on in," Mrs. Cacic called from the kitchen.

Maja held her girls' hands as they followed Divac back toward the table.

"Mrs. Cacic, we just wanted to check on you and see how you were doing, considering what today is," Maja said. She looked down at her two daughters fidgeting but still clinging to her hands.

"What is today again?" Mrs. Cacic asked.

"It is the anniversary of—" Maja began.

"We don't need to remind Mrs. Cacic," Divac said. "She has had a long day. We'll be going now."

Divac turned to leave, but Mrs. Cacic refused to dismiss them.

"No need to tip-toe around that subject," she said as she eyed a spoonful of the soup. "That was seven years ago. I haven't forgotten, but I have moved on. That chapter of my life is over, and there's no need to mourn his passing any more."

"How is your soup?" Maja asked.

"It is still so hot that I have not tried it. Here," Mrs. Cacic said, lifting a spoon up to Maja. "You try."

Divac's eyes widened as he watched Maja guide the spoon toward her mouth. He had to think quickly.

"Anja, stop doing that to your sister," Divac said as he reached for his youngest daughter. As he did so, Divac bumped Maja to draw everyone's attention elsewhere before he knocked the bowl onto the floor, spilling the soup all over her.

"Oh, I'm so sorry," Divac said. He snatched a napkin off the table and blotted up the soup that was strewn across the floor.

"Jovan!" Maja said. "What on earth are you doing?"

Divac didn't look up as he cleaned. "Just an accident. Maybe you should get Mrs. Cacic another bowl of soup while I mop this up."

"Good idea," she said before returning to their apartment with the girls.

When Divac finished, he stood and inspected his work. "I am really sorry about this, Mrs. Cacic. I am afraid I have brought you more trouble for your day."

"Trouble is forgetting to feed my dog," Mrs. Cacic said. "Offering me a bowl of chicken soup only to knock it on the floor is just rude."

Divac decided he needed to leave—and leave immediately.

"You never answered my question, Mr. Divac. Can you help me with my pipes?"

He met her gaze as her eyes narrowed.

"Maybe later, but I need to get going, Mrs. Cacic. It was a pleasure visiting with you. And I hope you enjoy the soup Maja brings you. I have some girls who are in desperate need of a bath."

"We need to talk soon," Mrs. Cacic shouted as he exited into the hallway. Just outside the door, Maja was returning without the girls but with another bowl.

"That was fast," Divac said.

"The soup was already warm as it had been simmering on the stove for quite a while."

"Didn't you want to talk to me about something?"

She nodded. "Just wait until I get back. This should not take long."

Divac rushed back to their apartment but stopped short of the door. On the knob hung a red ribbon, the signal that Divac's contact was waiting for him in the lobby with instructions for a specific mission.

He slipped inside and grabbed his coat. "I will be back in five minutes."

"Where are you going?" Maja called. "We need to talk."

"I need to get something for Mrs. Cacic."

He closed the door and hustled toward the stairwell before making his way to the lobby. A man sat on a bench against the wall, reading the *Novosti,* Belgrade's most popular newspaper. He proceeded to fold up the paper, set it down, and then walk away. The two men never made eye contact as they passed one another.

Divac settled onto the bench and picked up the paper and found a note tucked inside. The message was simple: Deliver the package tomorrow at noon.

That means I need to leave tonight.

Crossing the border into Italy and making his way to Venice wouldn't be easy, but he was paid handsomely for his efforts. At some point, he figured he would have enough to start a new life somewhere else with Maja and his girls. But until that day arrived, delivering documents for the CIA was the most lucrative work he could ever have. The inherent danger associated with each mission was reason enough to give him pause, but he shrugged it off. He was convinced his life was at risk every day, subject to the whims of the SDB.

Later that evening, after putting his girls to bed, Divac took a phone call from someone at the CIA. Whoever called never said anything, but Divac faked his end of the conversation. The ruse was designed to quell a full-scale interrogation from Maja.

When Divac hung up, he informed Maja he had to leave.

"You have to go to work? At this hour?" she asked.

He nodded. "I have to go when called upon. You know I have to take every job I get."

She sighed. "Fine, but when will you be back?"

"I am not sure, but don't wait up for me. I will see you tomorrow."

Divac put his coat on and zipped it up, hoping that his last statement would actually be true. But he knew it was likely a lie. Getting to Venice and back in less than twenty-four hours wasn't impossible, just highly improbable considering the time required to slip past the heavily guarded border. Divac figured he would be lucky if he returned home in forty-eight hours, resigning himself to deal with the consequences later.

* * *

A HALF HOUR LATER, Divac slid into the front seat of a half-empty produce truck driven by his friend Miroslav. After the CIA successfully recruited Divac to work for them, he learned Miroslav was one of the major reasons why. Easy access to a route that led him to the Yugoslavian border without raising much suspicion was valued greatly in the espionage world.

"What are you doing this time?" Miroslav asked.

Divac wagged his finger. "You know I cannot tell you any details, Miro. Just drive."

Miroslav turned the key in the ignition, and the engine chugged to life. He turned on his headlights and eased onto the gas.

"Do you think you can get me a job with the CIA?" Miroslav asked.

Divac handed Miroslav an envelope containing a few hundred dinars. "If you quit your job, I lose this position. Don't you like getting all this extra money for doing nothing."

"Risking my life by letting you ride with me is hardly *nothing*."

Divac shot Miroslav a sideways glance. "All you have to do is drive while you let me sit here. It is about as close to nothing as you can get."

Miroslav shrugged. "When the bullets start flying, you might think differently."

"No one is going to shoot at us, Miro. You can be so paranoid sometimes."

"Is that why two SDB agents are following us right now?"

Divac leaned forward and looked at the side mirror. "There is no one behind us."

"But there was."

Divac chuckled. "Oh, Miro. You want to be a spy so badly. I promise you that it is not as exciting as it looks."

"Narrowly avoiding death every day may not be exciting to you, but it sounds very exciting to me. It is far more thrilling than driving a produce truck back and forth between Belgrade and Ljubljana all the time."

"If you want more money, just ask for it. I can always put in a request."

"How about you request that I join the CIA. I know where a few SDB agents live, and I could sneak into their homes and—"

"You would not be breaking in to anyone's house," Divac interrupted. "The real reward you receive is knowing that you may have prevented something terrible from happening."

"Or you may have caused it."

Divac furrowed his brow. "You are confusing me, Miro. Earlier you sounded like you wanted to join. Now you sound like you want to turn me in to the SDB."

Miroslav waved dismissively at Divac. "Just forget I said anything."

In the early morning hours, Miroslav pulled into the parking lot of the produce company. He parked near the loading docks and locked up the truck.

"Do you want me to take you to Vrtojba on the border?"

Divac shook his head. "I have made other arrangements."

"You mean I am not your only driver?" Miroslav asked.

"Goodbye, Miro. I will bring more money next time."

Miroslav shuffled off to his car, kicking rocks along the way. Divac stood motionless in the parking lot until Miroslav disappeared into the night.

Divac glanced around the grounds before heading down the street for his final rendezvous. Two men crammed into a small two-door car pulled up next to him.

"It sure is a nice night for a drive," the man in the passenger side said after he had rolled down his window.

"Only if you don't like the stars," Divac fired back.

The man got out and pulled the seat back, making room for Divac. After climbing inside, he slid to the middle so he could hear both men equally.

"You need to keep your head down," the driver said. "The SDB is patrolling the area, and they saw us go by a few minutes ago. And there were only two of us in the car. If they spot a third head, they will pull us over."

Divac remained in the hidden position for most of the hour and a half ride to Vrtojba, barely speaking another word to his new acquaintances.

Once they reached Vrtojba, the car veered off the highway and onto a washboard dirt road. The vehicle vibrated as it jutted along for a couple miles until finally stopping along the edge of a farmstead property. They only safe way over the border was on foot.

"Are you sure this is a good idea?" Divac asked. "What if the owner of this house comes outside with a shotgun?"

The man who had been driving eyed Divac closely. "They said you were paranoid. And they weren't lying either."

As they took a slight detour through the farmyard and toward the border, Divac heard a click and froze. A few seconds later, a light on the outside of the farmhouse flickered on.

The voice of an elderly man called out into the

night, demanding to know who was out there. Divac watched the farmer's shadow against the light before breaking into a dead sprint. The farmer pulled the trigger, setting off a *boom* that reverberated through the trees.

The other two men caught up with Divac, all pumping their arms as hard as they could while churning across the farmyard. Divac placed his hands on the fence in front of him, effortlessly jumping over it before continuing his pace. The other two men fell behind shortly but caught up when Divac hesitated as he approached the dense forest.

"Which way?" Divac whispered.

"Follow me," the driver said.

Divac anchored down the third spot in the single file line of men racing through the woods in an effort to cross the border into Italy. One by one, the men jumped over fallen logs and scampered across shallow streams trickling past. They were making good speed until the sound of a siren roared in the distance, followed by the incessant braying of hounds.

"We need to move more quickly," the lead man said.

Divac held his hands near his face to protect it from getting slapped by twigs and branches snapped back by his two companions. His heavy breathing resulted in billowing wisps of air exiting his mouth. Divac's legs started to burn, but he ignored the sensation as long as he could. When he finally decided to take a short break, sweat trickled down into his eyes, stinging them.

"Let's go," the other man yelled over his shoulder.

"You mustn't stop for any reason."

Divac resumed his breakneck speed until sweeping floodlights caught them all off guard. Some shouting followed by gunfire erupted in the stillness of the forest.

Divac watched numbly as the two men who had accompanied him stumbled to the ground. He wanted to help them, but he knew he would get caught and possibly be shot on sight. Against his wishes, Divac pressed on.

He reached a clearing and managed to find his second wind as he raced toward the border, which was marked by a large wooden fence topped with barbed wire. Once there, he wasted no time in grasping a wooden post and beginning his ascent. Then out of nowhere, bullets peppered the area around him.

With a deep breath, Divac moved methodically up the fence until he reached the top. He flung himself over it and shimmied down to the other side.

Dawn was breaking by the time he cleared the woods and reached the town of Gorizia, Italy, just in time to buy a train ticket to Venice.

During the ride to Venice, Divac wondered what secret message he was passing along. Any temptation to sneak a peek was quelled by the fact that the package contained a wax seal—and that his work for the CIA provided him with the majority of his income. Divac wished he could live a normal life, one devoid of worrying about money or the SDB agents who swarmed the streets of Belgrade. He simply wanted to enjoy his family.

One day we'll escape all of this.

For the rest of the trip, he was lost in his thoughts, considering the ramifications of Mrs. Cacic being an SDB assassin and recognizing that the two men who were gunned down at the border could've just as easily have been him.

The hissing of the brakes and the inertia that came with the train stopping at the Venice station jolted Divac back to reality. He still had a job to do.

A half hour later, he was walking near the designated dock, searching for his contact. Divac stepped to the edge and noticed a gondola careening around the corner. The gondolier was belting out his rendition of "Moon River", which was the signal.

Divac flagged the gondolier down and eased his way into the vessel. After a short ride through the canals of Venice, he got out of the boat, leaving the package behind.

Divac walked a few meters before glancing back over his shoulder to notice a man with an eye patch and a hook for a hand climbing into the same gondola. With a wry smile, Divac turned back around, knowing the drop had been successful.

CHARLES PRITCHETT TIGHTENED the metal casing around his hook. Over the past week, the rattling created by several loose screws had started to bug him. Whenever he made sudden movements, the aluminum parts ground against themselves, resulting in a high-pitched squeaking noise—and he was fed up with it. He was so focused on fixing his hand that he didn't look up when he heard someone rapping on his office doorjamb.

"Is everything all right, Pritchett?" Ed Maddux asked.

Pritchett's star recruit had been a wonderful edition to the Bonn station and was progressing more rapidly than Pritchett ever anticipated.

Pritchett ignored the comment as he guided the small Phillips-head screwdriver into place before tightening the final binding.

"Are you engaging in some sort of surgical procedure?" Maddux asked again after Pritchett failed to respond.

Pritchett grimaced as he gave the screw one final

turn and then set the driver down his desk emphatically.

"Now maybe I won't sound like the tin man on the yellow brick road when I walk down the hall next time," Pritchett said as a victorious smile spread across his face.

"Dorothy would be proud," Maddux cracked.

Pritchett leaned back in his chair, giving off the impression that he was relaxed. Yet mentally, he was anything but at ease.

"Have a seat," Pritchett said, gesturing toward the chair across from him.

Maddux eased into the chair. "How was your trip to Venice?"

"Uneventful, thankfully. But the message I received was full of *interesting* information. And by *interesting*, I mean frightening, terrifying, and horrible."

"That good, huh?"

"Harvey Cordell, one of our top agents in Belgrade, compiled a dossier on a new program the Russians have been working on, Operation *Serp i Ogon*, or Sickle and Fire."

"Certainly sounds intimidating."

Pritchett shook his head. "Intimidating is what you do when you aren't sure you can win a fight. This new operation takes more of a scorched earth approach. Apparently the Russians have been working for years to develop what we're calling super assassins, agents who can perform incredible feats with jaw-dropping precision. Just imagine snipers who would likely win gold medals at the Olympics in the 100-meter dash. Rugged, tough, damn near indestructible. At least that's how Cordell described them."

"Why are they in Belgrade?"

"It's a less conspicuous place to launch these people into the world. We don't have the manpower to watch around the clock the facility where the Russians are grooming these assassins."

"Has he seen any of these alleged super assassins?"

Pritchett nodded. "He photographed a training session in the woods an hour outside of Belgrade. It's hard to tell from the pictures just how talented these men and women are, but Cordell swears it's one of the scariest things he has witnessed since joining the agency. But that's not the worst of it."

"I can't believe it being any worse."

"Well, for me it is. Supposedly I'm on a short list of targets assigned to certain assassins, particularly one codenamed Medved—the Bear."

"What do we know about him?"

Pritchett sighed. "Not much. But we believe he is responsible for killing one of our agents in Italy this past weekend with a butcher knife."

"I hadn't heard about this."

"Yeah, it's not exactly the kind of report we want publicized. We worked with the Italian authorities to keep it quiet. Our agent was in the country under the guise of working as a liaison at the embassy, but his real job was communicating with Italian intelligence regarding a few lingering groups from the war."

"Did he make any mistakes?"

"Not that we were aware of, which is disconcerting to say the least. I'd sleep much better at night for the sake of our agents knowing that he made a grave error in judgment or some misstep along the way. But if the truth is that we have a mole within our agency, God help us all. None of us will ever be safe again."

Maddux swallowed hard. "What kind of mole are we talking about?"

"We can't be sure, but it certainly seems like someone is feeding this information to the Russians on a platter—and they're eating it up, wasting no time to take action."

"So what's our next step?"

"At this point, we're just going to continue to gather information and wait."

"Business as usual then?"

"That's the directive I received. But if there's a mole out there, I want to ferret him out. None of us will be safe if someone in the agency is disseminating our secrets."

"Just let me know how I can help."

Pritchett nodded before dismissing Maddux.

The news of an agent's death always created uneasiness around each station. To Pritchett, the angst was almost palpable. Staff members wore dour demeanors and spoke in solemn tones, almost hushed whispers. Every agent knew the inherent danger associated with working for the agency—for some that was part of the allure of working for the CIA. But when a threat became imminent, the idea of death became sobering and terrifyingly real.

Pritchett shuffled around the office, attempting to keep up moral. He tried to lighten the mood with a few jokes he'd heard over the weekend while out at his favorite *biergarten*. But it didn't take long for him to realize that no amount of jocular banter could return the atmosphere to normal. For the time being, this was the new normal: anxious, frightened, and vulnerable. Worst of all, Pritchett felt helpless to stop it. Whoever this Medved was needed to be found and terminated, which wasn't an easy task given that they knew little about his whereabouts. If he was responsible for the death of the agent in Italy, Medved was likely long gone, moving on to the next target. And Pritchett only hoped his name wasn't next on the list.

Later that afternoon, Pritchett sifted through the report he'd received via the CIA's civilian contact in Belgrade. The microdot on the message Pritchett collected was filled with more information on Medved, though none of it was actionable intelligence. There were several more pictures as well as notes about his habits at the training facility, including the fact that he was left handed. But when it came to finding material useful in tracking down this alleged Russian super assassin, Pritchett was striking out.

Pritchett tidied up his desk before heading home. He varied his routes home, often deciding by the flip of a coin so as not to fall into a routine. By the time he reached the street, dusk had fallen. He preferred the sparse light over both broad daylight and darkness. He maintained a swift gait as the street lamps twinkled on.

He checked behind him before taking a sharp right turn down a dimly lit portion of his walk home. Usually unflappable, Pritchett jumped when a black cat screeched before scurrying in front of him.

I don't need any more bad luck than I already have.

He steadied his breathing and continued along the sidewalk. In the distance, he could hear the cacophony caused by impatient drivers, skidding tires, and a few people yelling—all normal sounds in a big city.

Then he heard something that made his heart race.

Footsteps. Plodding and methodical footsteps.

Whoever the mystery person was, he was certain about where he was going—and his pace increased every few seconds.

Pritchett rounded the corner and ducked under a stoop jutting out from an apartment building. Crouching low, he watched the man walk past, head down and eyes forward. Never once did he glance back over his shoulders.

Maybe I'm just being paranoid.

Pritchett let out a sigh of relief and scolded himself for getting so frightened by the mere sound of someone walking behind him. However, he wasn't sure how long he could walk out in the open in such a vulnerable position with Medved still running rampant.

When Pritchett entered his apartment, he collapsed onto his couch and loosened his tie. He tossed his hat onto the chair across from him and closed his eyes. This kind of thing wasn't supposed to happen within the CIA. Leaks, targeted agents, a collapse of intel gathering systems—the entire system the agency had created to maintain its presence right under the nose of its enemies suddenly felt tenuous at best.

Pritchett was lost deep in his thoughts when his phone rang, snapping him out of the mental doldrums he had entered. He staggered across the room to the receiver and answered.

"This is Pritchett."

"Cordell is missing." The voice belonged to Walt Kensington, the Belgrade station chief.

Pritchett scowled. "Come again."

"You heard me. Cordell went missing two days ago."

"Are you sure about this?"

"He always checks in, even when he's on an assignment of such a delicate nature. But it's been over forty-eight hours and nary a peep."

Pritchett cursed under his breath. Cordell was a highly decorated agent and had taken out several KGB assassins in the past. He was as skilled as anyone in the agency. For him to go missing, Pritchett realized, the intelligence gathered on Medved presented more than a theoretical thereat.

The Russian super assassin was very real—and if all the intel was accurate, he was coming for Pritchett soon.

III

ED MADDUX WASN'T SURE he should've been allowed to enjoy his position with the CIA so much. It didn't take long for the romanticized idea of espionage to wear off, but Maddux latched on to other facets of the job that he relished more than he should have. He delighted in deceiving rival agents, though that was more necessary for survival than anything else. Utilizing the latest technological gadgets supplied to him by Rose Fuller were also moments he savored. But the travel—as devoid of glamor as it was at times—was a perk he couldn't imagine relinquishing after less than a year of serving in Bonn.

His latest assignment satiated his growing wanderlust in both style and location, a dinner cruise around Venice, Italy.

With Medved still on the prowl, Pritchett opted against traveling to an unknown location without the kind of security required to keep him safe. He feared entering the public with an entourage was a sure way to paint a giant target on his back for the Russian super assassin. Pritchett often expressed how much more comfortable he felt in Bonn rather than other European cities, citing his familiarity with the area as an advantage should a pursuit ensue. More exit points, more hiding spots, more obstacles for a discreet assassin to take him out. But someone had to convene with Walt Kensington to get the scoop on what was going on in Belgrade and what the station chief had learned. This wasn't the kind of conversation they could have over the phone, and with the messy state of affairs in Belgrade and the assassin hunting Pritchett, a face-to-face rendezvous was the best solution. Maddux's ability to arrange a business meeting in Italy with relative ease resulted in him getting tapped to go and gather all the intel Kensington had to offer on the Russians' super assassin program as well as the disappearance of Harvey Cordell and any news on Medved.

Following a short flight to the Venice Airport, Maddux caught a taxi to the docks before boarding a water taxi. Sharing the service with a handful of other passengers, Maddux found a seat along the outer edge. He closed his eyes, basking in the warmth of the autumn sun. He moved his head into the path of the periodic sea spray that splashed upward whenever the boat hit a large wake. The salt water felt good against his face. Since moving to Bonn, he hadn't had a chance to explore the rivers around the city and see if any would make for a good location to row. But just the smell of the water and the feeling he got while bounding across the waves awakened his desire to row again.

The boat's engine whined as it skipped across the water. After what felt like half an hour to Maddux, the captain throttled back on the power and eased the vessel into the busy harbor. He found a dockhand standing on the edge and calling out to every captain that passed by.

One of the attendants in the boat slung a rope toward the young man, who wrapped the twine around the dock cleat at the front before following suit in the back. Once everyone agreed the ship was secure, the passengers were escorted off. Maddux watched the captain tip the dock attendant, who thanked the captain before disappearing.

While Maddux wanted to take in more of the city, he didn't have much time before the dinner cruise was scheduled to depart. Pritchett and Kensington agreed on the location because a ticketed event on a cruise ship gave them some modicum of control in a territory foreign to both Kensington and Maddux. And such a move made sense to Maddux, though he wondered what might happen if a KGB agent learned of this proposed engagement. Would Maddux and Kensington be easy targets in a confined area with no legitimate escape routes? Maddux hoped he wouldn't have to find out the answer to that question.

When Pritchett explained the details of the meeting, he omitted the most vital information: what dinner cruise they would be taking. Keeping the location a secret was the best way to ensure that if either the Bonn or Belgrade station contained a mole, he wouldn't be able to tip off Medved or the KGB about it. Maddux walked to an address he'd been given, which happened to be a small hotel. Once there, he asked the bellhop a coded question. He slipped a piece of paper out of his pocket and handed it to Maddux. He read the note: **Il**

Marlin Volante, 19:00. After inquiring about directions to the floating restaurant, Maddux learned it would take no more than fifteen minutes to walk there.

With plenty of time to kill, he decided to walk around the city for a half hour before making his way to the restaurant. The savory smells wafted into the street, causing Maddux to grow hungrier by the minute. He crossed a bridge and watched a gondolier navigate along one of the canals. Eventually Maddux reached the Il Marlin Volante and asked about the cruise's route during the meal.

He learned that the majority of the cruise would occur in the Venetian Lagoon, circling the area. However, the dockhand explained that the captain intended on navigating beyond the barrier islands and venturing briefly into the Adriatic Sea, mostly so tourists could claim they had traveled there. That was the portion of the cruise that concerned Maddux the most, leaving them trapped for some period of time.

A small crowd was already gathered, but it grew rapidly over the next five minutes. Maddux looked up to see waiters and waitresses scurrying around the ship's open deck while making final preparations. The large boat had three decks, with the two lower decks stretching out farther than the previous one. Maddux refocused his attention to the growing number of patrons, trying to identify any possible miscreants. Most of the people came as couples, both old and young but all wide-eyed with anticipation of the romantic evening ahead of them. A few large groups were also present, though their topic of conversation was oriented around the large wine selection on the menu. Maddux didn't notice anyone else boarding solo and wondered if Pritchett should've sent a companion.

Maddux trudged after the diners, who had been instructed to board the ship. Before he could brood over the potential misstep any further, he heard a man behind him speak softly.

"One if by land, two if by sea," the man said.

"Paul Revere was lucky the airplane hadn't been invented yet," Maddux said, completing the verbal clue.

"Nice to meet you," Walt Kensington said. The Belgrade station chief shook Maddux's hand but didn't wait for a response, instead turning to the pair of women flanking him.

"And who are these lovely ladies?" Maddux asked.

"This is Sophia and Francessca," Kensington said, gesturing toward each one as he said their name. "They will be accompanying us tonight. I figured you wouldn't mind these dames joining us."

The two women forced a smile and nodded in unison. Sophia joined Maddux on his left.

"Shall we?" Kensington said, gesturing toward a table set for four.

They all sat down, the two women next to one another in order to give Kensington and Maddux space for a private conversation.

"Do you know these women?" Maddux asked as he studied the ladies who were already lost in a conversation.

"The less you know, the better."

"But what if—"

Kensington put his hand out, signaling for Maddux to stop. "I know this might seem careless to a young buck like you who just entered the profession, but you're going to have to trust me on this one. If someone believes I am passing secrets, the last thing I want to do is blow my cover by bringing two women from my station. For all I know, my entire unit is blown."

Maddux shrugged. "Well, you're the expert. I know you didn't rise to the level of chief by acting carelessly in the field. I will gladly defer to your judgment."

Kensington took a deep breath and then exhaled slowly through his nose. He closed his eyes and tilted his head back.

"Don't you just love the smell of the open water?" Kensington asked as the boat lurched and embarked on its short journey. "It always smells like adventure wafting through the air."

Maddux scanned the group of diners, all engrossed in conversation. "I prefer solid ground."

"Weren't you in the Navy?"

"I'll try not to take offense—or wonder how you missed that in my file."

"Take it easy, Ed. Just a little small talk appetizer before we commence with the main meal. But I guess it runs in the family. Your father was always wound up tight like you are right now."

A man in a tuxedo strode out onto the middle of the deck with a microphone and welcomed all the guests. He explained how the dinner was structured and what would be served during each course.

Maddux stared at the host and watched his lips move but wasn't listening to a word he said. Kensington's off-handed comment set Maddux's mind awhirl again.

"You knew my father?" Maddux asked.

"I've run into him several times over the years. He became a valuable ally for us while he was working in Belgrade several years ago."

"Can you tell me what happened to him?"

Kensington sighed. "Look, I know that had to be tough just losing your dad overnight, but I can't say everything I know. He was deep into some highly classified projects, stuff you don't have clearance for. And frankly, not many people do. Your father was getting us information from behind enemy lines, and the fewer people that knew about him, the better."

"And he's still there?"

"I already told you that I can't say anything else about it," Kensington said. "But we came here to give you some classified information that happens to be a more immediate need."

"Medved," Maddux said, nodding. "What do you know?"

"To be honest, what I know isn't much. Cordell was the one who was handling all the surveillance on the KGB training camp for these super assassins. But here's what I can tell you—Medved is dangerous and likes to stalk his prey."

"Seems like he's been working quickly."

A waiter eased in between them and filled their glasses with wine. Kensington swirled his drink around and put it up to his nose to inhale the aroma before taking a sip.

Maddux waited until the waiter was out of earshot before nodding at Kensington to continue.

"Maybe, but that's predicated on the fact that you

believe Medved is the only one of these special agents prowling around. Medved just happened to be the most notorious of the class of agents Cordell had been following. And if his intelligence was correct, the KGB wasn't going to release all of them at once—but that doesn't mean they didn't release two or three."

"So you think there might be more out there?"

Kensington nodded. "I'm inclined to think that Pritchett is being stalked by Medved."

"Right now?"

"Even as we speak."

Maddux narrowed his eyes. "And you didn't warn him?"

"Of course I warned him," Kensington said, bristling at Maddux's insinuation. "As station chiefs, we all know we have a target on our backs if our cover gets blown over here. But he's at an even greater risk now."

"What makes you think Medved is stalking Pritchett?"

"Just a hunch really. But from what Cordell told me about Medved, that's how he was trained. These super assassins will be tough to defeat in hand-to-hand combat, but their true intent is to remain ghosts, which means even their kills need to look like a natural cause or naturally accidental."

"Anything else I need to know about Medved?"

Kensington raised his index finger and forced a smile before reaching into his back pocket. He produced a small black-and-white photograph of a man.

"I went back through Cordell's effects after he went missing and found an undeveloped roll of film. He'd described Medved to me many times, so when I saw this photo, I knew it was him."

Kensington pushed the picture closer to Maddux, who picked it up and studied it closely. As he studied it more closely, Maddux's eyes widened, and his mouth fell agape.

"Are you sure this is Medved?" Maddux asked.

"Ninety-five percent sure," Kensington said.

"Do you know who this is?"

"I already told you it's—"

"No," Maddux snapped. "I mean, do you know who this person actually is?"

Kensington shook his head. "Should I?"

"That' s Gunnar Andersson, one of the top race car drivers on the Grand Prix circuit."

"Maybe you should be the one briefing me."

"I'm just in shock. Going to the KGB's training facility seems like a brazen move for someone who has a world famous face for his exploits on the race track."

"Perhaps he was planted there, recruited to do exactly what he's doing. Racing gives him unfettered access to countries that might otherwise be difficult to penetrate. But a driver just walks into the U.S. or any of her allied countries with a simple flash of his passport and a friendly wave."

"That might even be more frightening than the fact that super assassins exist in the first place."

"It's a dog-eat-dog world out there now," Kensington said. "Nobody is pulling any punches any more."

"Well, if this is Medved, you might be right about him stalking Pritchett. I read an article in the paper that said Andersson would be in Bonn testing out a new engine for his sponsor ahead of the Monte Carlo Grand Prix."

"Pritchett needs to be extra careful then, maybe even get out of town for a while."

"You know he's not going to do that," Maddux said. "The man is a battle axe personified. One eye, one arm, and a sharper edge than you."

"Sounds like some slick marketing slogan, Maddux. You don't happen to know anyone who does that for a living, do you?"

Maddux forced a smile. "I might know a guy."

Kensington placed a packet on the table. "It's not much, but I found a few more extra notes that Cordell took while staking out the training facility. Something in there might help you get a leg up on Medved."

The waiter returned with their plates and glanced down at the documents. With a quick glance and a slight nod, he gestured for Maddux to move the papers to make room for the salad plate.

"*Scusa*," Maddux said.

The waiter nodded approvingly and placed the food on the table.

"As we like to say here in Italy, *buon appetito*," the host said over the microphone.

Delighted "oohs" and "ahhs" filled the crisp evening air, followed by the clanking of forks against dinnerware. Maddux and Kensington returned their focus to their companions for the evening, making small talk as they continued their meal.

After dinner, Kensington asked Maddux to take a walk with him on the deck.

"We'll only be just a few minutes, ladies," Kensington explained.

The two men descended to the middle deck.

Kensington stopped about halfway down and stopped to look out across the water.

"She's beautiful, isn't she?" Kensington said.

Maddux furrowed his brow. "Who? Francessca?"

"No, no. Venice. Just look at her, twinkling in the night against a rippling mirror at her feet. There's no other city like her in the world."

"That's because most people are sane enough not to found an entire city on water."

Kensington kept his gaze affixed on the city in the distance. "I would argue that most people don't have the ability to imagine something like this. They see water and they think, *no way. It's not happening.* But that's not what a visionary does. They see opportunity even when it doesn't readily present itself."

"Are you a visionary?"

"I'd like to think of myself as one, but I'm a patriot above all else. If you live behind the iron curtain for as long as I have, you realize what our country has is something really special. We're not subject to the whims of dictators. Even a wave of dissent seems toothless in our great republic."

"No country is insulated from corruption. While our republic might be great, it's still flimsy. That's why we're here, isn't it?"

"We're all here for different reasons," Kensington said. "Some of us just want to see the world. Some of us truly want to protect our democracy. Some of us are looking for the right opportunity. What are you really here for?"

"It's clear why I'm here—to protect all the wonderful privileges our great nation has afforded her citizens."

"Is that the only reason?"

Maddux eyed him carefully but didn't say a word.

"You see, I have this theory that you're only here because you want to find out about what happened to your father," Kensington continued. "And in my book, that makes you dangerous. You're here for selfish reasons, cloaking yourself in the flag."

"Maybe my quest to find my father pushed me into saying yes to the agency, but I can assure you that my intentions are honorable here."

"Let's hope so," Kensington said. "I've found that men who join for ulterior motives find themselves adrift after a short period of time. And any agent who isn't moored to the ideals and principles that we're fighting to protect becomes susceptible to treason."

"I appreciate your concern and the pep talk. But you don't have to worry about me."

The two men continued to stare out across the water at Venice in silence while the boat rocked gently with the waves. Kensington pulled out a pack of Marlboros and offered it to Maddux.

"No thanks," Maddux said. "From what I understand, those things will kill you."

Kensington chuckled as he flicked his lighter and lit his cigarette.

"There's something I wanted to—" Maddux said before stopping abruptly as a bullet whistled right past him and stuck into the wall behind him.

"Move it," Maddux said, pushing Kensington forward.

Both men hunched low and moved quickly across the deck. Another bullet shot past Maddux, this time hitting the deck just inches away from his feet.

"Come on," Maddux said. "You've got to move quickly."

They rounded the corner before they heard a final bullet smash the glass on the corner room.

"What the hell was that?" Maddux said once they reached the other side of the ship. They both sat down, sinking to the deck with their backs against one of the outer walls.

"Someone must've figured out who you were," Kensington said.

"Our waiter," Maddux said. "Had to be him. But how did he get off the ship?"

"Perhaps it was, but we don't have time to solve foolish mysteries. You need to get that information back to Pritchett before we all become targets. I know he'll know what to do with it."

Sophia and Francessca almost strolled right past them before stopping.

"Gentlemen," Sophia said, stooping down to look them in the eyes, "are you all right? You look a little shaken, Mr. Maddux."

"I'll be fine," he said before rising to his feet. He offered his hand to Kensington, who took it and quickly stood upright.

"Where did you two go? We were looking all over for you," Francessca added.

"I went for a smoke," Kensington said.

"Those things will kill you," Sophia said with a wry smile. She dug into her clutch and pulled out a pack of cigarettes, holding it out to Kensington. "Want another one?"

Maddux had seen enough of Venice from the

water. He was ready to get back to Bonn and discuss what he learned with Pritchett. And Maddux wanted to do it immediately. Whether the KGB actually had super assassins was still a debatable notion; the fact that Maddux was being watched wasn't.

Someone knew who he was—and they were trying to kill him.

CHARLES PRITCHETT ADJUSTED his eye patch and rubbed his forehead as he studied a report from the Berlin office. As if launching a few super assassins into the wild to track down CIA agents wasn't enough, Pritchett also had to deal with a burgeoning problem from the Berlin embassy where an agent discovered a KGB listening device embedded in the ambassador's desk. No one knew exactly how long it had been there or who had been compromised as a result, but Washington was up in arms over how such a thing could happen.

Pritchett sighed as he read the painful report regarding how the KGB likely planted the device. With each passing paragraph, he wondered if this incident might absolve The Thing as the KGB's greatest triumph over the U.S. in the intelligence war. Regardless of where the incident fell among the CIA's greatest blunders, someone had to deal with the fallout—and as dicey of a situation as it was, it still paled in comparison to the looming threat from the KGB's latest weapon of super assassins.

When Pritchett first heard that term, he scoffed.

"Who gets to decide who is super and who's not?" he asked in a meeting. His question was met with a terse response and a folder slid down the table toward him. The report inside documented several key U.S. allies in the business sector who had been vocal in their opposition to Russia. Within the past week, three men were dead—all under suspicious circumstances.

"This sounds like some drummed up conspiracy, like all those nuts who think JFK was killed by some shooter on the grassy knoll or that the CIA was orchestrating the entire thing. It's just absurd."

"Aren't you the one who says there are no coincidences?" one of the agents at the table asked. "If you truly believe that, you can't dismiss what's happening out there. These assassins might be the best we've ever encountered."

Pritchett glared at the agent, unappreciative of getting called out in such a public manner. But the man was right—Pritchett didn't believe in coincidences. If he was honest with himself, he simply didn't like the fact that the KGB had a leg up on the CIA, not to mention that he was being targeted.

He scratched his chin with his hook and scanned the room. "In that case, you work up several responses we can make to mitigate these assassins, both foreign and domestically, and I'll pass them along."

After the meeting, Pritchett retreated to his office, where he seethed in silence. He wasn't alone for more than a minute before Maddux rapped on the door.

"Yeah," Pritchett grumbled.

"Got a minute, boss?" Ed Maddux asked, poking

his head inside the room.

"So you made it back," Pritchett said.

"Barely. Someone started shooting at me and Kensington while we were out on the water."

"One of those assassins made you?"

"Apparently. We both got out of there as quickly as we could. If it hadn't been for the choppy waves that night, I might be shark chum right now."

"Have a seat," Pritchett said, gesturing toward the chair across from his desk.

Maddux closed the door and sat down across from Pritchett.

"Tell me what you learned," Pritchett said.

"We've got our work cut out for us, that's for sure. But I think I know who the super assassin is who is supposedly coming after you."

"How the hell did you figure that out?"

Maddux reached into his pocket and produced the picture Kensington had given him. "Do you recognize this fellow?"

Pritchett picked it up and squinted with his good eye at the image. After several seconds, he shook his head.

"Who is that?"

"Gunnar Andersson of Grand Prix fame."

Pritchett grunted. "I'm not a fan of racing. It's a silly sport, if you can even call it that."

"Be that as it may, the picture Kensington found from the training ground contained a photo of this guy doing plenty of amazing stunts. He's a real athlete, not just some guy who can mash a pedal to the floorboard and steer a car."

"Kensington is sure this is the guy?"

Maddux nodded. "Not a hundred percent, but close enough. He placed it at ninety-five percent."

"Those are good odds."

"Even better than that is the fact that Andersson is in the area for the next few days testing his car at Nordschleife."

Pritchett took a deep breath. "In that case, I have an idea. While you were gone, I started to wonder about the mole. I know it's not you, but I can't be sure about anyone else—*anyone*. So, let's take an opportunity to flush out Medved and the mole at the same time."

"What do you propose?"

"We tell the entire team of my whereabouts tonight for a dinner engagement. I'll be there as a guest of the U.S. ambassador as we discuss more investment opportunities here in Germany with the mayor of Bonn in a private room at a local biergarten. You'll be the only one there, working undercover to see if Medved shows up."

"And if he doesn't?"

"Then we'll know the mole isn't in this office. But if he does make an appearance, you'll have to apprehend him. We'll figure out the rest from there."

"Sounds like a plan."

* * *

LATER THAT EVENING, Maddux took up a position in a vacant apartment across the street from the restaurant where Pritchett was dining with the ambassador, Richard Billups, and the mayor of Bonn, Dr. Wilhelm Daniels. Pritchett's official cover was that he was a business consultant for the U.S. embassy in Bonn and worked closely with Billups to develop opportunities for

American investment. Pritchett's resume was a complete fabrication, though verifiable to outsiders due to the CIA's extensive counterintelligence division. Daniels had been a close ally with President Kennedy and even hosted the popular leader on one occasion.

While the conversation appeared jovial from Maddux's vantage point, he marveled at how Pritchett was putting on quite a show.

Pritchett looks like he's really enjoying himself.

But Maddux knew better. The old man's stomach was undoubtedly wadded up in knots as he awaited the infamous Medved to strike, possibly killing him. Yet, no one appeared even close to Andersson's stature. Even out on the street, the restaurant was devoid of any suspicious activities.

Maddux checked his watch periodically, until the trio arose from the table and headed for the door. Rushing downstairs to keep an eye on them when they hit the street, Maddux emerged from the apartment building just moments before Pritchett and company.

Still no sign of Andersson—or anyone resembling him.

Maddux kept his distance from Pritchett for several blocks until the station chief was all alone. Maddux hustled to catch up.

Pritchett spun around just before Maddux arrived.

"Well, did you see him?"

Maddux shook his head and kept walking, trying to keep pace with Pritchett. "I think you're free and clear."

"Maybe, or maybe they were just waiting for another opportunity."

"If Andersson is Medved and we have a mole in our office, there would've never been a better time to strike than at that meeting. He could've killed three high-profile officials, all adversarial toward Russia, in one fell swoop."

Pritchett shook his head. "I don't think that's how these assassins work. An attack like that would engender sympathy for us, backfiring on the KGB.

"If he's going to kill you, it needs to be done discreetly."

"So, what are you doing here talking with me?"

Maddux slowed his pace as Pritchett did. "I'm here a part of your security detail. We wanted to use you as bait, not throw you to the wolves."

"Bear," Pritchett corrected. "You're throwing me to the Russian Bear."

"You know what I mean."

Pritchett nodded. "This was all an experiment anyway to find out if we had a mole."

"And draw out Medved."

"Well, the two are inextricably linked."

"Not necessarily. Medved could come after you later. Maybe he just had you under surveillance tonight."

Pritchett stopped. "Look, we can conjecture all night long. The bottom line is nothing happened, even when Medved supposedly had a great opportunity to score a big win for the KGB."

Pritchett resumed walking, increasing his pace. Maddux hustled to keep up.

"I think we need to know for sure if Gunnar Andersson is Medved before we draw any conclusions about what happened tonight."

"What do you suggest then?"

"The Monte Carlo Grand Prix is coming up. It'd be a good excuse for me to go to Monaco and speak with some of the drivers on behalf of Opel. We may need some new drivers for an upcoming advertising campaign we're about to embark upon."

"Why not go visit Andersson at Nordschleife?"

"That'd be too conspicuous. I can't even pretend to have a legitimate excuse if I go out there tomorrow."

"You've convinced me," Pritchett said. "Go make it happen."

* * *

PRITCHETT AMBLED HOME with Maddux a few meters behind. Once Pritchett hit the door to his apartment building, he entered and didn't even turn around to see were Maddux was. That snub was by design since they didn't want anyone else to think they were acquaintances.

Pritchett trudged up the steps, dropping his guard as he considered all the different possibilities surrounding Medved's true identity and the uncertainty felt by leading a CIA station that may or may not contain a mole. But Pritchett snapped back to the present when he heard the clicking of heels against the cement steps behind him.

Footsteps in the hallway were normal for this time in the evening as weary workers straggled home. But Pritchett could identify almost every man living in the building by the sound they made while walking up the stairs. With his vision dulled after the loss of sight in one eye, he experienced a heightened ability when it came to his hearing. And whoever was behind him, he knew it wasn't one of the regular tenants.

Pritchett reached the landing that led to his floor, but he continued upward. Losing a tail was a skill he excelled at. If he had exited the stairwell on the same level as his apartment, he would've made it easier for the mystery stalker. Instead, Pritchett went to the top floor before dashing down the hallway toward the other stairwell on the opposite end of the building and descending to his floor.

The plan worked as Pritchett had hoped. He unlocked the door to his apartment and hustled inside. Collapsing on the couch, his heart was still thumping from the escape.

Was he being tailed by Medved? Pritchett couldn't be sure. All he knew was that whoever was behind him was a newcomer.

He took a deep breath and waited for the phone to ring.

Five minutes later, he jumped when Maddux called.

"Did you see him?" Maddux asked.

"I couldn't make him out," Pritchett said. "It was too dark, but the man didn't look as tall as Gunnar Andersson. It's not much, but that's what I gleaned from the situation."

"He gave you the slip?"

"Big time. I'm not sure he suspected he was being watched until he reached the top flight of stairs. He stopped abruptly, breaking the cadence I was using to match my footsteps with his."

"Did you see him leave the building?"

"I watched him vanish along the sidewalk. I tried to follow, but he blended into a handful of workers going home for the day. Sorry, chief. I did everything I could."

"No worries. I might have to mix up my routine even more for the next few days until we catch him."

Pritchett hung up, resisting the temptation to venture over to the window and watch the people of Bonn scurry home like he did every night. A creature of habit, Pritchett would have to stay on his toes at least until they knew Andersson was out of the area and back on the racing circuit hundreds of miles away somewhere.

Based off Maddux's comment, Pritchett wasn't convinced Andersson was Medved. But maybe Andersson was the assassin assigned to target Pritchett.

While the plan Pritchett executed was designed to answer some nagging questions, he ended up only raising more.

THE NEXT DAY AROUND NOON, Maddux left his office at Opel to check in with Pritchett. Maddux wanted to debrief about the previous night's plan and what went wrong, but he also wanted to deliver some news.

"They're sending you to Belgrade? What on earth for?" Pritchett asked.

"Our embassy there set up a meeting between the Yugoslavian minister of commerce and Opel in an attempt to discuss building a plant in Belgrade to create some new jobs," Maddux said.

Pritchett furrowed his brow and looked at his coffee in disgust. "But why do you have to go? That seems out of your area of expertise."

"I'm part of the advance team that goes to these types of meetings. However, if you don't think it would be in my best interest, you could make a phone call."

Pritchett waved dismissively. "No, it'll be fine. I'm afraid of how it might look for you if someone has suspected you as a spy. But just be careful."

"I will," Maddux said. "It might give me a chance to meet with Kensington again and get an update on the search for Cordell."

"That would be helpful, but if you do meet with him, make sure it's a place where you'd naturally see him, like at the embassy perhaps."

* * *

THE NEXT MORNING, Maddux boarded a plane for Belgrade with the rest of the team members from Opel. When they landed, they were met by a liaison from the embassy who escorted them to their hotel. As they were unloading their luggage, Maddux asked the embassy worker to pass a note along to Walt Kensington.

"I'll see what I can do," the man said. "Mr. Kensington didn't come in this morning."

"Is that unusual?"

"He has an irregular schedule, but he always makes an appearance in the office for at least some portion of the day. I'll make sure he gets this, no matter when he comes in."

Maddux grabbed his bag and headed to the registration desk to check in. After getting his room key, he took the elevator upstairs to settle in. He spent the next hour preparing for their dinner meeting with Yugoslavian government officials scheduled for later that evening.

At the restaurant, Maddux engaged Yuri Gaspar, the Yugoslavian minister of commerce, in a wide-ranging conversation. They discussed the most recent Olympic games as well as the revolution of personal transportation thanks to the booming automobile industry.

"I really believe our country's economy could be revitalized if we had more transportation solutions," Gaspar said. "There are certain communities that are thriving because their economy is insulated. But the rest of Yugoslavia—even here in Belgrade—suffers."

"And you think making the people more mobile will change the economic outlook?" Maddux asked.

"It would not hurt. Right now, the Yugoslavian people have two choices for their lives: move or leave the country."

"From what I understand, the second option doesn't really exist."

Gaspar nodded. "Some people make it out alive, but we are losing some of our best and brightest, lured away by the success offered beyond our borders."

Maddux wanted to ask Gaspar about the draw of freedom as well but decided against stirring the pot any further.

"Well, if there's one thing I know about Opel, it's that we make some damn fine automobiles at an affordable price. If we partner with you, we'll put people to work and give the great people of this country more opportunities with better mobility."

Gaspar laughed heartily before tipping back the rest of his wine glass. "Now that is what I like to hear."

Maddux excused himself from the table to use the restroom. Once inside, he was met by the embassy liaison who had picked the team up from the airport.

Maddux eyed the man closely. "If anyone sees us talking—"

"Don't worry," the man said. "I've been watching and when I saw you get up, I made sure the restroom stayed empty."

"So, why are you here?" Maddux asked as he washed his hands.

"There's been a development with Mr. Kensington."

Maddux arched his eyebrows. "A development?"

"Mr. Kensington never came in today. We sent someone by his apartment, but he never answered. We spoke with several other agents at the Belgrade station, and they said he was supposed to be there for a meeting with them but never showed up."

"So, what are you trying to say?"

The man looked down. "Mr. Kensington is missing."

THE PHONE JANGLED on the nightstand, awakening Maddux from what was a restless night of sleep. His return flight to Bonn was scheduled for that evening, giving him nothing but time to kill. He'd wanted to sleep in, but Pritchett put an end to that idea.

"Is it really necessary to call me this early?" Maddux asked, rubbing his eyes as he tried to focus on the clock.

"It's 7:30," Pritchett said. "Why would you be complaining? Are you recovering from being out on an all-night bender?"

Maddux grunted. "I wanted to after the news I got last night."

"I heard yesterday evening, too. I'm starting to think we have other problems now aside from the one we already had."

Maddux scanned the floor for a pair of pants. He understood Pritchett's reticence to speak freely on the phone and dropped into speaking in code. The SDB could be listening—and likely was.

Pritchett continued. "Just focus on your tasks today, and we'll address these issues tomorrow after you get back. Don't do anything stupid that you'll soon regret."

Maddux sat on the edge of the bed and pulled his pants on. He crossed his fingers before answering. "Don't worry. I've got plenty of work to keep me busy. I'll stay out of trouble; that much you can count on."

"Good luck, and safe travels," Pritchett said before he hung up.

Maddux uncrossed his fingers. The act was juvenile, but it made lying to Pritchett somewhat easier. No matter what Maddux did with his fingers, he never had any intention of staying put and playing it safe—not when there were KGB assassins on the loose and gunning for agency operatives and station chiefs.

Maddux donned his hat and jacket before heading toward the CIA's Belgrade station. He picked up on a pair of SDB agents tailing him and decided to duck into a coffee shop. He ordered a cup and drank half of it before going to the restroom. But instead, he slipped into the back alleyway and continued along. Certain that he had lost the men after walking several blocks, Maddux hailed a cab. He asked to be dropped off two blocks from the location. He wove through several blocks, ensuring that he wasn't being followed again before entering the station through a secret entrance. But what he found there shocked him—the building was empty.

No matter what station Maddux had visited during his short stint with the CIA, he had always found at least one person managing some type of activity. Whether a listening station or an agent filing a report, someone always had the lights on. But not today.

Maddux went through the small office space to verify the vacancy.

"Hello? Is anyone here?" he called out.

Nothing.

After a few seconds of not getting a response, he looked for Walt Kensington's office. He found it after a brief search and jimmied the lock open. Maddux went straight for the filing cabinet behind Kensington's desk. He rifled through folder after folder, looking for anything else that the Belgrade station chief might have failed to give to him.

Still nothing.

Maddux was about to break into Kensington's desk when the name on a file folder at the back of the drawer gave him reason to pause. The name John Hambrick was scrawled in a black marker across the tab. Maddux's eyes widened as he opened the folder and studied the one lone document inside—a photo of two men, Kensington and Maddux's father.

Maddux squinted as he held the picture closer to his face. The pair stood on a dock outside an industrial type building. Combing the photo for any other details that would give away their location, Maddux stopped when he noticed a sign hanging in the background behind them. He recognized the place almost immediately, but it wasn't in Belgrade.

Kensington knew my father better than he let on. Why would he lie to me?

Maddux pondered a hypothetical list of reasons why Kensington might want to conceal the true nature of his relationship with Maddux's father.

Maybe Kensington was trying to protect me, or maybe they are still working together and he's not authorized to tell anyone. Or maybe he doesn't like my father personally and is carrying out a vendetta against him.

There were no easy answers, especially when Maddux didn't even know the right questions to ask. All he could do was keep in mind the fact that Kensington downplayed the nature of his relationship with Maddux's father. Maybe it meant something; maybe it didn't.

Maddux snapped back to the present when he heard voices outside the door. He wasn't sure if it was an agent returning from an assignment or the SDB. Either way, Maddux didn't want to stick around to find out. Even if a friendly face emerged around the corner, he didn't want to have to explain his presence and why he was rooting around in Kensington's office.

Maddux stuffed the photo into his jacket pocket. He methodically shut the filing cabinet and scrambled to open the window. Climbing out onto the fire escape, he shut the window before scurrying down to the ground. He hustled back to the sidewalk and walked briskly toward a nearby bus stop.

Once he was on board, Maddux breathed a sigh of relief and pulled the picture out once more to look at it.

Walt Kensington, where are you?

VII

JOVANE FOLLOWING AFTERNOON, Maddux strolled into the CIA offices in Bonn and approached Pritchett. The station chief was pacing around his desk, scratching his chin and staring at the ceiling.

"Is every thing all right in here?" Maddux asked, gingerly poking his head into the room.

"I'd be a lot better off if all our agents weren't disappearing," Pritchett said as he narrowed his eyes and shook his head.

"What happened this time?" Maddux asked.

"Another agent in Belgrade gone. Apparently he was nabbed off the street in a brazen kidnapping by the KGB. Of course, they're disavowing any knowledge of the event or their participation in it."

"So there were witnesses?"

Pritchett shook his head. "Not exactly, but we know that this is how the KGB operates, especially in conjunction with SDB. If they've pulled a stunt like this once, they've pulled it a thousand times over. Their mission is to gain some leverage on us."

"Do you think they're making a play to get one of their agents back? An invaluable scientist perhaps?"

"That thought crossed my mind. So far, none of the kidnapped agents have wound up dead, which leads me to believe that they have plans for them. If they were going to kill those men, they would've done it by now."

Maddux stared out the window. "I can't argue with that sound logic. However, these men don't respond logically. If they keep taking our people, they're going to have more than just a bargaining chip at the negotiation table. In fact, they might strong arm us into doing their bidding for them."

"There's little doubt this needs to end right now."

"What do you want me to do about it?" Maddux asked.

"We need to flip the tables on them."

"And how do you propose we go about doing that?"

"Gunnar Andersson—if he's one of the KGB's super assassins, we need to capture him. We can force the Russians to agree to some sort of understanding."

"You think they'll go along with that?"

Pritchett shrugged. "Right now, it's better than hiding out and waiting for our agents to vanish. And who knows? Maybe we can flip Andersson."

"Use him as a double agent?"

"That's one option we have if we can't get the Russians to agree to anything else." Pritchett stood. "Now, there's only one thing left to do."

"What's that?"

"Convince Opel to send you to Monaco."

Maddux smiled wryly. "I think I can handle that.

I've always wanted to go to the Monte Carlo Grand Prix. I'm sure I can come up with some excuse to let them send me. Maybe scout out a potential location to film a commercial."

Pritchett nodded. "Make it happen."

"There's just one more thing," Maddux said.

"What's that?"

"I'm not sure this is the kind of mission I should go on alone. I'll definitely need some help."

"What kind of help? Brawn or brains?"

"I doubt any amount of muscle will overpower Andersson if he's the one we're after."

"In that case, take Rose."

Maddux exited Pritchett's office with a hint of a grin.

VIII

MADDUX'S SUPERIORS PUT UP some resistance to his idea of traveling to Monaco. They expressed concern about him racking up a large tab on the expense account while staying in one of Europe's playground for the wealthy. But he convinced them that the trip to scout shooting locations for television ads was worth the investment.

The next morning, Maddux visited Rose Fuller in the bowels of the Bonn station. She wore a knee-length skirt and had her hair tied up in a bun. Maddux's footsteps arrested her attention as she looked at him over the top of her glasses from across the room.

"I've been expecting you," she said.

"And I've been looking forward to visiting you again down here," Maddux said as he surveyed her vast work area.

He picked up what looked like a piece of coal and tossed it up in the air several times.

"Don't do that," Rose said as she hustled across the floor toward him.

Maddux furrowed his brow and ignored her.

"What does this thing do?"

She enclosed her hands around his and gently pried the rock from him. She set it down on another table and gave him a sideways glance.

"It's a bomb, Ed."

"A bomb?" he asked, mouth agape.

"Yeah, the kind that goes boom if you tinker with it."

Maddux stooped down and studied the object. "That little thing right there will explode?"

"It would blow your head off if you were that close to it when it detonated."

Maddux studied the rock for several seconds before Rose walked up behind him and grabbed him as she yelled, "Boom!"

Maddux jumped back several feet. He glared at her while she giggled with delight.

"Oh, so you think that's funny, do you?" Maddux asked.

"We need moments of levity around here," she said, gesturing toward a nearby table. "Do you see all this here? Poison, bombs, guns—I spend most of my time creating devices that will either kill or severely injure opposing spies. I think I'm entitled to a laugh at your expense every once in a while."

"Maybe I'm just not in the mood today. We have serious work to do."

"Yes, we do," she said, gliding across the room toward a worktable. "We need to get you equipped to plant a bug as well as open any envelopes our target might receive without him realizing someone has read his mail."

Maddux settled onto a stool on the other side of the table from Rose. "Show me how all this works."

Rose began a fifteen-minute tutorial on how to work the gadgets. The bug planting kit was designed for any agent to stealthily plant a bug in a wall or furniture without getting detected. Small hand drills along with other devices eliminated any visual clues that someone had been drilling into a surface and leaving a microphone. The mail-reading tool cut a small hole into an envelope before the user turned the handle, wrapping the letter tightly around a shaft and pulling the note out without breaking the seal. Once the letter had been read or photographed, it could be reinserted without as much as a wrinkle made.

"And do you have my credentials?"

"Of course I do," she said, handing him a badge that identified him as a reporter for *The Miami Herald.*

"Miami?" he asked as he read the name. "Why not New York or Los Angeles or Chicago?"

"The Miami area is fond of open wheel racing," she said. "The nearby city of Sebring has a big Grand Prix event every year and recently hosted the U.S. Grand Prix. And Miami once had a great grand prix track before the Great Miami hurricane wiped it off the map. To top it all off, the newspaper wasn't sending anyone, so I fabricated everything for you. You'll be able to walk right in."

"And take pictures?"

"In broad daylight."

Maddux sighed. "Well, that's unfortunate. I was looking forward to using one of these cameras." He glanced down at the table at the pack of Marlboro cigarettes that hid a camera inside.

"You'll get to use that camera, too," she said.

"We're going to need some photos to verify that Gunnar Andersson is the same man in the photographs that Kensington gave us. People can look similar in pictures, but when you see them in person, they can look completely different."

"Anything else I need to know?" Maddux asked.

"Yes," she said, nodding slowly. "Don't do anything stupid that will get both of us killed."

"What makes you think I would do any such thing?"

She cut her eyes toward him before looking away but remained silent. "I'll see you in Monaco."

* * *

MADDUX DONNED A LIGHT JACKET for the breezy spring weather in Monaco. Aside from serving as a warm barrier against the wind blowing in off the Mediterranean, an extra layer of clothing provided an inconspicuous place to hide all the gadgets Rose had loaded him down with. As he secured each kit and device she had given him, he considered the term pack mule would be more appropriate than spy in this case. If any security guard attempted to pat him down, Maddux conceded that he would be exposed as something other than a reporter.

Maddux slid the final—and most crucial—element into his pocket. The pit pass Rose replicated for him would allow him unfettered access into the pits the day before the race and would accomplish both his objectives. The first thing he needed to do was plant a bug in Andersson's vehicle. For a man who was on the move all the time, the open wheel racer would likely be somewhere in the vicinity of his competition car. And Pritchett suggested that placing the bug in the driver's side door would give the CIA an opportunity to capture candid conversations between the suspected Russian super assassin and his handlers.

After pulling into the parking lot designated for the press, Maddux gave himself a final once over before getting out. He snatched his briefcase off the passenger side seat and ambled toward the gate. In the distance, he could hear the roar of the engines as well as the waxing and waning of cars making warm-up laps. The race was still several hours away, but Maddux felt the anticipation building as he neared the entrance.

Another man dressed in a dark suit with a press credential hanging from a lanyard around his neck nodded at Maddux as he waited approval for entry. The crush of reporters attempting to get in created a bottleneck.

"Just be patient, all of you," snapped an elderly gentleman seated on a stool just outside the track entrance. "We can only go one at a time, but you will all get in eventually."

The reporter who had wandered up behind Maddux and joined him in line groused about the procedure.

"They do this every week," the man said, his voice rising as he spoke. "You'd think that by now they would've figured out how to handle things more efficiently. But, oh no, checking each individual reporter and verifying their press credentials five different ways means that we all have to stand out here waiting when we should be in there doing our jobs."

The man's open complaint was met with head nods, which spurred others to share their stories of long

wait times and general incompetence in ushering reporters through the gate. Maddux wondered if all news-
papermen regarded themselves as so self-important or
if it was unique to those covering the Grand Prix race
circuit.

The line moved along systematically, but Maddux
was inspected and granted access within fifteen minutes,
a wait which he deemed reasonable. He waited on the
reporter behind him who had been griping so loudly inside the gates.

"Excuse me, but can you tell me where the pits
are?" Maddux asked.

"You must be a rookie," the man answered. "What
paper are you with anyway?"

"The Miami Herald."

"The Herald is covering the Grand Prix now? Now
that's surprising." The man offered his hand to Maddux.
"Bill Newton with The New York Times."

While Maddux's employers sent him to Monaco on
official business, his CIA duties required an alias.

"Paul Miller," he said. "And, yes, I am new to this,
so you'll have to pardon my ignorance."

"We all had a first time," Newton said, gesturing to
his left as he started walking in that direction. "The second I walked into a stadium and smelled the burning
rubber and watched the cars zip past me, I was hooked.
I still remember it like it was yesterday."

Maddux hustled to keep up with Newton's swift
pace. "Do you talk with the driver's much before the
race?"

"That'd be a rookie mistake," Newton said. "Most
of the guys don't like to be bothered while they're

getting ready. But a few of them don't mind. It really just depends on who you're wanting to interview."

"What do you know about Gunnar Andersson?"

Newton took a deep breath and stroked his chin as he stared off in the distance. "That guy is an enigma. I've spoken with him on several occasions, but I can never really get a read on him. Is he in it for the love of racing? Or does he just love the money? Not that it really matters, but I've found that the ones who love the sport, the competition, the thrill of it all—they're much more open than the men who would be doing something else if it weren't for all the fame and money associated with the sport."

"And where does Andersson fit in?"

"That's what I mean about him being an enigma— he doesn't seem to fit anywhere. He's nice enough when I've spoken with him in the past, but I don't know if he's seeking glory, fame, and riches or if it's all about the money."

"Thanks for the heads up."

"Oh, sure. Any time. If you ever need anything while you're covering the sport on the circuit, just come find me. I'll be happy to give you the scoop on any procedures that you might be unsure about."

"I appreciate that," Maddux said.

Newton stopped. "Now, the pit gate is straight ahead right there," he said, gesturing toward the opening in the chain link fence. "That guard's name is Monty, and he's still torn up about the Dodgers leaving Brooklyn, so don't mention anything about baseball and you'll be fine."

"I can't thank you enough," Maddux said again.

"It's nothing. Go have fun. Today's gonna be a hell of a race."

Maddux proceeded to the gate and had no problems getting inside the pits. Monty was friendly and asked Maddux for his opinion on who was going to win the race.

Maddux shrugged. "I have a hunch about Gunnar Andersson today."

Monty laughed, bordering on a guffaw that attracted the attention of several people passing by.

"Andersson? Are you out of your mind? He's always in the middle of the pack. No way he's going to win today. What would make you say such a thing?"

"Like I said, it was just a hunch."

Monty looked down at Maddux's credentials again. "Okay, Mr. Miller. I'll be sure not to ask you again. I didn't realize The Miami Herald was hiring comedians as sports writers these days."

Maddux knew the likelihood of Andersson winning wasn't high, but it was a safe answer. Had Maddux listed any of the top drivers, he could've entered into a long debate about who might currently be the best driver on the circuit. And he didn't have time for that.

Weaving his way through the pits, Maddux found himself dodging hustling crew members every few feet. Tires were rolled along, engine parts were carted around, inspectors scurried from garage to garage in order to complete their pre-race check of all the cars. He was overwhelmed with the busyness before finally stopping and asking one of the crew members who nearly flattened Maddux with a tire about Andersson's garage.

"It's the one on the far end," the man said, pointing

across the pit area.

Maddux strode toward the garage but was stopped short by a pair of men standing guard, both wearing dark sunglasses.

"That's far enough," one of the men said in English with a tinge of an Eastern European accent.

Maddux grabbed his credentials and held them up so the man could read, but he didn't budge. "I'm with the press, and I'd like to speak with Mr. Andersson."

Neither guard cracked, both appearing to keep their gaze forward in the distance.

"My name is Paul Miller from *The Miami Herald*, and I'd like to conduct a brief interview with Mr. Andersson before it gets too close to race time."

"No interviews," the other guard said. "Now run along."

Maddux shrugged and started walking away before peeling back around and angling to get into the pit and get Andersson's attention.

"I don't think so," one of the guards said as he grabbed Maddux's bicep. The other guard followed suit as they lifted Maddux off the ground, turned him in the opposite direction, and launched him forward. Maddux stumbled as his feet hit the ground, but he placed his right hand on the ground to maintain his balance and keep from falling.

"And don't come back," the guard said when Maddux looked up at him.

Maddux looked down at his press credentials.

A lot of good this thing does me.

He dusted himself off and glanced once more over his shoulder at Andersson's garage. With the driver nowhere in sight and the two guards proving to be menacing, Maddux decided to regroup and consider another approach. He strolled past more cars, stopping to get a closer view of several engines with those racing teams that were more amenable to his presence in the garage. He was staring at a Lotus-BRM engine with his mouth agape when someone pat him on the back.

"This doesn't look like Gunnar Andersson's car," Rose Fuller said.

Maddux turned around to see Rose wearing a pit pass and camera draped around her neck.

"What are you doing in here?" he asked.

"Same as you," she said. "Covering the race."

"But as a photographer and a—"

"I know, I know—a woman. I have attracted more attention than I anticipated, but that shouldn't be a problem since I spend most of my time locked away in a lab dreaming up ways to kill, maim, or otherwise injure people with small objects."

"When you put it like that, it sounds like you're talking about The Three Stooges," he said.

"What I do is far less entertaining," she said. "But enough about that. Tell me how things went with Andersson."

They both backed away from the vehicle and walked together around the garage.

"He's got two men standing guard over his garage, making sure no one gains access to his pit."

"Are you kidding me?"

Maddux shook his head. "I was unceremoniously tossed aside when I tried to slip past them after they'd already denied me."

"Sounds like a challenge I would love to take on."

"Only if you're crazy."

Rose smiled. "I have my ways."

"Using one of your gadgets to incapacitate them is going to attract plenty of attention."

"Who said I'm going to use any devices?" she asked with a wink. "I have other ways."

"Fine. Do what you've gotta do. I'd just love to see how you could pull this off *and* get the bug installed in his car."

"I'll grant you that it won't be easy, but I can handle myself in the field. Sometimes there is no gadget that can replace a human."

Maddux handed her the bug kit and watched her walk away, her hips swaying from side to side. He'd never noticed her walk like that before. She looked back over her shoulder and winked at him again.

He smiled and huffed a soft laugh through his nose. "I hope this works."

* * *

ROSE HAD ENOUGH TRAINING to be a credible field agent, even if it was about her least favorite assignment. At one point, she had dreamed of becoming a spy, stealing ciphers, and traveling to exotic locations to satiate her thirst for adventure. But the work in the field wasn't fully satisfying. Manipulating people with mind tricks and outright lies made her feel slimy. Plus, she eventually discovered how much she enjoyed using her creativity to craft tools for spies that would enable them to rely less on manipulative tactics. At the time, making such a shift seemed like a noble thing to do. Eventually she concluded that nobility could only be ascribed through a person's actions, not simply by the omission of certain acts.

However, there were times when nobility wasn't part of the assignment and the only thing that mattered was results.

This was one of those moments.

She fluffed her hair as she walked away from Maddux and smacked her lips. In a public situation where an agent had to slip past a pair of guards, gadgets were of little use. Knocking out one or both men would only result in unwanted attention. And the CIA always preached the first rule in penetrating enemy lines was to do so without raising an eyebrow from other onlookers. The more one stood out, the more people would remember details about the scene. Rose wanted to be entirely unforgettable to everyone else around.

Approaching Andersson's garage, she identified the two guards who Maddux pointed out were standing a few feet apart, hands clasped behind them. Neither one of the men even glanced in her direction as she made her way toward them, instead appearing to stare off into the distance.

"Is Gunnar available?" she asked with a smile and a wink.

Neither of the men moved.

"What is this? Buckingham Palace? I said *is Gunnar available*?"

One of the guards turned slowly and looked down at her. "No, he's not."

"Tell him to come out here right now," she said. "I had a great time with him last night at La Rascasse, and I need to give him something. It's for good luck."

The guard returned to his previous pose, refusing to comply with Rose's request.

Rose crossed her arms over her chest and poked out her lip. "This isn't very nice. He promised me you two would let me pass."

"Perhaps Mr. Andersson changed his mind."

"Changed his mind? *Changed his mind?* Are you insane? We had an amazing time last night, and I'm confident if I would've stuck around long enough, he would've proposed to me."

"Proposed to you? As in marriage?" the other guard asked before breaking into a chuckle.

"That's right," Rose said. "Laugh it up. But I'm telling you he was on the verge of breaking out a jewelry box he had hidden away. I just know it."

"Lady, it's time for you to move along," the other guard said with a subtle head nod. "Mr. Andersson is happily married to a model and was with her all last night."

She unfurled her bun as her brown locks fell around her shoulders. Shaking her head slightly, she gathered up her hair again and retied it. She strode up to the first guard who had addressed her and poked him in the chest with her index finger.

"You're going to wish you let me in after I tell Gunnar to have you fired," she said, narrowing her eyes. "You'll be sweeping streets or taking out rubbish."

"I'm about to take out some rubbish right now," he said, peering down at her finger, which was still pressed against his chest. "I suggest you step back and be on your way."

Rose stamped her foot. "Not until I speak with Gunnar."

The guard looked down again at her finger before she withdrew it. Once she did, he looked straight ahead again.

"I'm not going to ask again," she said.

Neither guard responded.

"Fine," she said as she backed up slowly. "I don't need your permission."

As soon as the word *permission* came out of her mouth, she exploded forward, pumping her arms as hard as she could in an attempt to slip between the two men. However, just as she expected, they caught her. That's when Rose broke into her act.

She thrashed back and forth while she screamed, shaking so violently that her bun broke loose. Her hair twirled around her, shielding anyone from seeing her face.

"Put me down," Rose yelled. "Help! Help! These men are attacking me."

Almost immediately, they released her, placing her feet on the ground and backing away. She smoothed out her dress before sneering at them.

"Go ahead, lady," one of the guards said. "We don't have time for your games."

The other guard scowled and glanced at his colleague but didn't say anything.

"Don't worry," she said before taking a deep breath. "I won't be long."

Rose pulled her jacket taut across her waist and approached the enclosed tent near the back of the garage area. She poked her head inside and entered gingerly.

"I thought I told you not to disturb me," Andersson growled before he turned around. When he swung around in his chair to see who was standing in the entryway, the scowl on his face transformed into a warm smile.

"Well," he said, cocking his head to one side, "I guess we can make an exception for you, doll."

She forced a smile and took a seat at the table across from Andersson. He was polishing his gun.

"Smith and Wesson 41," she said, staring down at his weapon. "Nice choice."

Andersson continued polishing, pausing only to glance at Rose and flash a smile. "I like a woman who knows her guns. Do you shoot?"

"Only when I have to."

"In that case, I hope I don't give you reason to shoot me."

"Don't worry," she said. "I'm not armed. I just wanted to bring you something."

"What? You don't want an autograph? Or perhaps a midnight rendezvous after I'm crowned champion?"

Rose stared at him blankly. "What would your wife think about that?"

"*Ex*-wife," Andersson corrected. "And I doubt she'd mind since we haven't spoken in months."

"Regardless, I'm not interested."

"And why would that be, Miss —"

"Delilah Boneparte," she said, offering her hand.

Andersson took it and kissed it slowly and deliberately. "Those supple hands don't look like they should be firing guns."

"Like I said, I only fire out of necessity."

"Well, Miss Boneparte, you still didn't answer my question. Why would you not be interested?"

"I only came to drop off some information for you," she said. "I had to be discreet about it."

"And screaming and yelling outside my garage is how you define *discretion*?"

"My job was to deliver something to you—and failing to do so wasn't an option."

"I also love a woman who won't take no for an answer," he said, leaning across the table to take her hands.

Rose withdrew and wagged a finger at him. "Just because I don't take no for an answer doesn't mean I don't know how to say it and enforce it."

Andersson sat back down in his chair. "Hence your range practice."

She nodded. "Now, you're starting to get it."

"Well, Miss Boneparte, I suggest you make this delivery of yours in short order before I have to go out there and claim my crown."

She reached inside her jacket and produced a packet. She slid it across the table to him and stood.

"Leaving already?" he asked. "I didn't really mean that you had to go right away."

She walked over to his side of the table and took his face in her hands. "If we had all the time in the world, you still wouldn't have a chance with me."

As she turned away, he lunged for her, groping her rear end. Rose turned around and smacked him.

"Don't make me use my gun," she said. "All the information is there for your next target. Don't blow it."

She snapped a quick picture of him and exited the tent. The two guards didn't acknowledge her as she split them on her way out of Andersson's garage area.

Weaving her way back through the busy garage

area, she struggled to hear herself think over the roar of the engines firing up. Crews pushed cars toward the starting line as the buzz of the crowd had grown to a constant hum.

Eventually, she reached the media viewing area near the starting line and saw Maddux. She stood next to him but never acknowledged him directly.

"How'd it go?" he asked.

"I made the delivery and snapped his picture," she said.

"You make it sound like it was easy."

"It was."

"How were you able to get past the guards?"

"I have my ways," she said. "Now, let's watch the race. You know I'm always looking for ideas on how to make agent cars go faster."

* * *

MADDUX STOOD IN SILENCE, taking in the scene of the popular raceway that would snake throughout almost every nook and cranny in the tiny country of Monaco. He glanced at Rose, who seemed equally in awe of the atmosphere.

The drivers paused to wave at the crowd and posed for pre-race pictures as journalists from all over the globe scrambled to some of the more popular racers to snap a picture. Flashbulbs exploded amidst the cheers and anticipation building from the grandstands.

Once the drivers climbed into their cars and the press returned to their safety zone, the grand marshal welcomed the crowd and wished everyone good luck before dropping the green flag. The automobiles roared down the track to a thunderous applause from the onlookers as they rose out of their seats for the first lap.

Maddux enjoyed the atmosphere, drinking it all in as he took a break from his espionage duties. One of the reasons the chance to move overseas with his company—and the CIA—was for these moments. While his fascination with racing started at a young age, he never had an opportunity to witness such a famous Grand Prix until this assignment. As the cars zipped past, he imagined what a commercial might look like for Opel, rushing through the streets of Monte Carlo along the same path as the Monaco Grand Prix. If he could sell upper management on the impact a commercial filmed here would make, he might earn a return trip next year.

Rose kept her distance, meandering away from Maddux for a while to gain a better vantage point for photos. He kept an eye on her while he noted the leaderboard. Andersson was running his best race of the season, fending off several challenges from British drivers Jackie Stewart and Graham Hill and Swiss star Jo Siffert, who were all piloting British Racing Motors cars. Andersson's Ferari engine purred as he zoomed past, pulling away from the pack.

But on the final lap, a disastrous spin out on the 180-degree turn at Gazometre put Andersson in a hole he couldn't climb out of. Hill and Stewart sped past Andersson as he struggled to get going amidst the wave of cars enveloping him. By the time he returned to full speed, the race was over with Hill crossing the finish line first.

Maddux watched as Andersson climbed out of his car in disgust. He threw his helmet, and it spun on the road. For good measure, he kicked the helmet, sending it sliding into the pits and clipping one of the other drivers on the back of the leg. Andersson received an earful but ignored the verbal lashing as he marched toward his garage area.

Maddux followed the throng of reporters who gathered near Andersson's tent and waited for him to emerge.

"Well, that was interesting," Maddux said to Rose as she joined up with him again. "You must've given him one hell of a pep talk. He hasn't come close to winning a race all season."

"If he was trying to impress me, he failed," she said. "However, if I didn't know better, I would've guessed he spun out on purpose. He had been navigating that Gazometre turn all day long as if it was child's play. But then with the race virtually in hand, he spins out? Something didn't seem right about that."

"Did you see it happen?"

She nodded. "He overcorrected for some reason. It's like he meant to do it."

"Maybe he did—or maybe he was thinking about his next assignment."

"Makes no difference to me, just as long as he shows up in Barcelona like we planned."

Maddux smiled and nodded. "Let's hope so."

The reporters mobbed Andersson as he stepped forward to answer questions. The throng pressed upon him so hard that he had to move, stepping away from the car. Maddux glanced over to see Rose slipping a bug into the car's frame, which was already being partially dismantled. She used a small clamp to attach the bug to the inside of the driver's side door, almost invisible to anyone working on the vehicle.

"Think that'll hold?" Maddux asked Rose as she re-joined him at the back of the pack.

She shrugged. "Maybe, maybe not. But at least it's in place. Once he gets to Barcelona, we'll be able to monitor that bug around the clock. Until then, let's just hope no one notices it."

Maddux glanced over his shoulder and saw a couple men standing in the shadows. He thought they looked out of place, perhaps even Russian. After waiting a beat, Maddux turned to get a better look—but they were gone.

IX

BARCELONA, SPAIN

FOR THE TWO WEEKS FOLLOWING the Monaco Grand Prix, a lull occurred in the number of CIA agents who suddenly went missing. Pritchett, while concerned about serving as bait for Medved, found relief in the fact that the KGB had halted its aggressive nature. He considered that may have boded well for him if the plan failed and he was indeed captured by the KGB.

Maybe they'll let me live. As long as I'm alive, there's still a chance that I could escape from prison.

If he was being truly honest with himself, Pritchett realized that a CIA station chief—one serving in Bonn, Germany, no less—would be tortured to learn everything possible before unceremoniously killing him. Pritchett wasn't certain what part of his fate he feared more: the sudden end or enduring the torture. He decided that the best way to ensure his safety was to make sure the plan worked.

Pritchett walked along Las Ramblas, stopping to purchase a collector's edition of *The Ingenious Nobleman Sir Quixote of La Mancha* from a street vendor. While still admiring Don Quixote for his lofty aspirations, Pritchett still viewed the character as a fool. Yet in some ways, Pritchett felt an affinity with Quixote. Deep down, they both wanted the same thing: a better world. However, where the two diverged centered around methodology. Quixote wanted to ride into every situation armed, a provocation that would more often than not hurt his ultimate desire to help mankind. Pritchett discovered that a covert approach resulted in not only a far better success rate but also proved to result in better relations between the nations.

But Quixote never put himself in a scenario that Pritchett was preparing to walk into, the type where capture was a possibility.

Pritchett strengthened his mind and concluded that even if he did die, his death would be for the greater good. His death would have purpose. His death would have meaning. But he would still be dead.

Instead of dwelling on the potential outcomes, Pritchett decided to enjoy meandering along Las Ramblas. Every few meters, vendors vied for his attention, often begging him to purchase one of their products. The trinkets amounted to little more than a flimsy item that would be broken just hours after purchasing it. Pritchett was only interested in one thing: capturing Andersson and getting some straight answers for once.

* * *

MADDUX ARRIVED IN BARCELONA two days before the scheduled operation to catch Andersson. The trap laid in Monte Carlo was hopefully convincing enough that he would walk into it without questioning its validity. The CIA station in Budapest had narrowly missed catching one of the new Russian super assassins, but it did manage to gather enough intelligence on how these agents were being handled as well as the protocol for receiving operations. Rose's appearance in Andersson's tent at the Monaco Grand Prix may have been unconventional, but the information she handed to him was in line with the intelligence gathered on how missions were assigned. And if Andersson was Medved, he wouldn't hesitate to follow the instructions Rose delivered.

With little to do other than meet with Spanish law enforcement to ensure that everyone involved was on the same page as well as meet with a few potential drivers for a future Opel television commercial, Maddux had some free time. And he wasn't going to waste it in any of the tourist spots. He was going to go check out the address he'd found in connection with his father.

The Vallvidrera residential area of Zona Alta located northwest of downtown Barcelona struck Maddux as a likely place for a spy to live. Far away from the bustling city, any suspicious activity from enemy agents would be easy to identify.

Maddux glanced at the note in his hand to make sure he was at the right address. Spacious and guarded lots were common traits among most of the homes in Vallvidrera. Leafy vines wrapped around portions of the wall surrounding the property. A cast-iron gate provided the only glimpse at what was on the other side.

Terracotta tiles adorned the roof of the three-story beige stucco home. The terrace encircled the structure, which was flanked on both sides by a pair of *garitas*. Maddux studied the grounds for a few minutes, deciding the best way to approach the house. He feared buzzing the owner from the street might not result in any answers. By the time he decided to scale the wall, a delivery truck pulled up and a driver with a package pushed a button to alert the resident. Moments later, the gate swung open slowly and the driver walked the rest of the way to the front door.

Maddux seized the opportunity to gain easy access, slipping in before the gate closed. He followed the delivery man, hoping to get an audience with the resident. There were no givens that the owner would be the same as when his father had some interaction here. But Maddux was determined to track down every lead and see where it took him.

A bald man with a goatee answered the door. Maddux guessed the man was in his early 60s. His gravely voice boomed as he thanked the delivery man and looked up at Maddux.

"I'm sorry, sir, but we don't accept any solicitation," the old man said in Spanish. "That's why we have a gate."

Maddux stepped aside to allow the delivery man to pass along the cobblestone path but remained pat.

"I'm not here to sell you anything, sir," Maddux said in English. "But I do have a few questions for you."

Maddux cautiously approached the man, walking up the steps to the front porch. Maddux reached inside his coat pocket and produced a picture of his father.

"Do you know this man?" Maddux asked.

The man took the photo and studied it for a second then shook his head. "He doesn't look familiar," the man answered in English.

"How long have you lived here?"

"I can't remember the year, but it hasn't been too long, maybe seven or eight years."

That timeframe perplexed Maddux. Unsure of when his father was in Barcelona made it difficult to determine if this owner could've known Maddux's father or not. Based on the man's emphatic denial, Maddux was inclined to take it as the truth. But the location and house screamed *spy* to Maddux. That along with the fact that the man transitioned to perfect English without even a hint of an accent gave Maddux even more reason to resist making any snap judgments.

"Sorry to have bothered you," Maddux said, "but thank you for your time."

The man nodded politely. "Buenos dias," he said before shutting and locking the door.

Maddux strolled toward the gate but studied the surroundings with keen interest. The man would've been about Maddux's father age.

By the time Maddux reached the gate, the driver was still sitting along the curb in his truck.

"Can you tell me who lives here?" Maddux asked.

The driver shrugged. "I'm not sure," he said in a Spanish-accented English. "The packages I deliver here are addressed to a different person each time."

"How long have you been delivering here?"

"Once a week for the past ten years."

"And has that man always lived here?"

"As long as I can remember, he always answers the door."

"No wife or kids?"

"I cannot say for sure," the driver said. "But I meet his wife once. I have not seen her in a long time, maybe five years. I'm not sure what happened to her, but she's gone. Maybe the old man kill her, but no one knows for sure."

"Is there every any mail addressed to her?"

"Not since I stopped seeing her. It's like she disappeared from the planet without a trace."

"Have you noticed anything else unusual about this house?" Maddux asked.

The man glanced at his watch. "I'm sorry, sir, but I really need to get going. I have a lot of deliveries to make."

Maddux dug into his pocket and handed the man 500 pesetas. "Just one more question."

The man pocketed the money and exhaled slowly. "What do you want to know?"

"Anything fishy happening here?"

"Fishy?" the driver asked.

"You know, strange or unusual?"

"That is a constant. I can't tell you the number of people I have seen coming and going at that place. Today was one of those rare days where I actually had to ring the doorbell to be buzzed in."

"I appreciate your help," Maddux said, tapping the side of the man's truck door, signaling that their conversation was over.

Maddux continued along the sidewalk. He looked over his shoulder at the house, which seemed quiet from the road. Without any context with the address, he didn't know the significance of the address—or the people inside, for that matter. But his instinct told him the old man was lying.

* * *

THE OLD MAN picked up his phone and dialed a number. He always suspected he might get a visit from John Hambrick's son.

"Yeah," the man on the other end of the line said.

"I got a visit today from the kid," the old man said.

"Hambrick's kid?"

"Yeah, that's the one. What do you want me to do about it?"

"Depends on what you told him."

"I didn't tell him anything. He showed me a picture of Hambrick, and I told the kid that I'd never seen him before."

"This's a dangling thread."

"I know. Still want me to leave him alone?"

"For now. I doubt he knows anything. He's just grasping at straws at this point."

"But what if he starts to put it all together?"

"We'll cross that bridge when we get there—or if *he* gets there. He has many miles to travel before he starts to piece everything together."

"I could make it look like an accident."

"And raise his old man's ire? No thanks. Let's just leave it as is and deal with the kid if he starts to become a problem."

The old man hung up and ventured up to the veranda. He could still see the man walking down the sidewalk. He stopped and glanced back at the house, oblivious to the fact that he was being watched.

X

PRITCHETT ORDERED A SHOT of tequila and sat at El Rio Cantina in Barceloneta just a couple blocks from the beach. The quiet fisherman's quarter was in the midst of a transition into a more robust commercial area. But some quaint locales remained, establishments that only attracted local patrons. While new restaurants and taverns were being erected closer to the beach for tourists, a few streets away, Barceloneta was still lost in time.

Pritchett picked at his paella, unsure if he wanted to finish it or not. His stomach churned as he listened to the end of the Barcelona Grand Prix on the radio. He was hungry, and Maddux encouraged him to eat something.

"I wish I had never agreed to this," Pritchett said. "It's bad enough that I always walk around in fear of someone shooting me in the back of the head. But to invite someone to do it? It's sheer lunacy."

"It'll never come to that," Maddux said. "We have plenty of agents here who will take down Andersson."

"You still think he'll show?"

"If he is who we think he is, he'll most definitely make an appearance."

The announcer calling the race became excited, sharing with listeners that Jim Clark had taken the checkered flag. Pritchett listened for several more minutes before the final standings were announced. Andersson finished fourth from last place.

"Just my luck," Pritchett said. "Andersson stunk it up today. It means he was either thinking about killing me all day, which distracted him from his driving, or he will be ticked that he performed so poorly that he'll be looking to let off a little steam."

"Either way, it won't matter," Maddux said. "He's never going to get off a shot."

"Forget it," Pritchett said before tossing back the shot of tequila. He screwed up his face, pursed his lips, and closed his eyes. After a moment, he exhaled and blinked hard.

Maddux chuckled and slapped Pritchett on the back. "See, all you needed was some tequila to put you at ease."

Pritchett went back to eating his paella. "I guess I shouldn't be so nervous about this. After what I read about what these KGB-trained super assassins can do, I don't want any part of them."

Maddux glanced at Pritchett's hook. "Andersson should be more afraid of you than he knows. I'm sure you know how to use that thing."

Pritchett held it up and smiled as he studied. "I used to wield this as a weapon back in the day. I prefer to manage things from behind a desk these days. I thought the last action I'd ever see in the field was in

New York at the World's Fair."

"Life has a funny way of surprising us sometimes, doesn't it?"

"To say I'm surprised would be an understatement."

"I don't care how scared you are," Maddux said, "the fact that you have enough courage to even suggest you would be willing to do this tells me that you will finish this assignment."

"As long as I finish it in one piece with Medved in custody."

"If he comes here, I guarantee you that will happen."

"Good," Pritchett said as he shoveled another forkful of food into his mouth. "That's what I want to hear." He motioned for the bartender. "Another shot of tequila, *por favor.*"

Pritchett spun around on his barstool to an empty restaurant. One of the agents at the racetrack a half-hour drive away was monitoring Andersson's status. The minute he drove off the grounds, Pritchett and the team would be notified.

The plan was simple as far as CIA operations went. With the agency renting out the entire restaurant for a private party, it planned to populate the restaurant with its agents along with assisting Spanish law enforcement. Once Andersson entered the tavern and asked the bartender for Pritchett, one of the lead agents would signal to the others to apprehend Andersson. The whole process figured to be quick and painless, especially if everything happened as planned before any weapons were drawn.

But Pritchett knew nothing ever went as planned, which was why he was still anxious.

When Maddux got up to go check in with the rest of the team assembled, Pritchett was left alone with his thoughts. He considered ordering another shot of tequila but decided against it. If something went awry, he wanted to have the full complement of his wits. He briefly contemplated his future with the agency, wondering if it might be time to call it a career. After all, he had plenty to be proud of and a list of accomplishments that could fill several books. But the idea was fleeting, pushed out by an even more terrifying thought to Pritchett than being used as bait to catch a Russian super assassin: *What would I do if I quit the agency? I belong in the world of espionage because that's who I am—I'm a spy.*

Pritchett ceased his self-loathing and determined not to wallow in his fear any longer.

And you're a damn good spy, too.

A few minutes later, Maddux whistled from the doorway and alerted Pritchett to the fact that Andersson had left the track and was in his car.

"Let me know when you're certain he's heading our way," Pritchett said.

Over the years in joint operations with the FBI, Pritchett had captured more than a dozen KGB spies on U.S. soil. Conceived and led by Pritchett, Operation AE Black Hat was responsible for the arrest of six KGB operatives in an intricate spy ring that had its tentacles reaching into the Pentagon and FBI. He caught another KGB agent offering to pose as a double spy by laying a trap for him comprised of faulty intelligence. When the agent was caught feeding intelligence back to the

Kremlin, he had an unfortunate accident one afternoon while trying to make some toast in the bathtub. Two spies he caught were traded back for one embassy worker and a U.S. Senator's son. Over the years, Pritchett made a name for himself in Soviet intelligence circles.

Yet operating in Europe was still relatively new for him—and not easy, even for an experienced officer as himself. Making the right call while conducting missions on foreign soil often consisted of balancing political relations while keeping the country's intelligence agency happy. This exponentially increased the level of difficulty for each exercise.

"He'll be here in five minutes," Maddux reported from the doorway. "You ready?"

Pritchett didn't turn around, waving his hook in the air instead. "I was born ready."

Pritchett slipped his hand into his coat pocket and gripped the blade. It was there just in case things went sideways. If Andersson somehow evaded capture and was intent on killing Pritchett, he at least wanted to be able to defend himself. A gun would've been preferred, but with a sharp hook in one hand and a knife in the other, Pritchett could deliver a lethal cut in a matter of seconds. He could recall at least three times where he ripped through the jugular of attackers with his hook, the slash they never saw coming. Even with one hand, Pritchett still considered himself competent in hand-to-hand combat, competent enough that he could survive a fight against an equal opponent. However, he joked that he held elite status within the agency for hand-to-hook fighting.

Nevertheless, Pritchett hoped his interaction with

Andersson wouldn't get that far.

"He just parked outside on the street," Maddux reported.

"Damn," Pritchett muttered. "I was hoping he wasn't Medved."

"We've got your back, sir," Maddux said. "Just stick with the plan."

The plate of paella was long gone, replaced in the past few minutes by *crema catalana*. Pritchett dipped his spoon into the dessert and savored the bite.

"If things go south, at least I had a fantastic final meal."

"Sir, you're not going to die today. Not if I can help it," Maddux said.

"I know," Pritchett said. "I'm going to be fine."

He slammed his hook into the table and used his other hand to dab the corners of his mouth with a napkin.

"Now get to your position, Maddux. We've got a super assassin to snare."

Pritchett took another bite of the dessert and waited. If everything went off without a hitch, Andersson would be in the private room in a matter of seconds. And Pritchett didn't want to waste any of the dessert.

He waited and trusted that his team was prepared to corral Andersson and eliminate any threat he might pose.

Less than a minute later, Pritchett heard an unfamiliar voice.

"Mr. Pritchett?" a man said.

Pritchett turned around slowly, laying eyes on Gunnar Andersson.

"Yes?"

"Do you recognize me?" Andersson asked.

Pritchett pursed his lips. "You look familiar. Should I know you?"

"Never mind that. There's something I need to tell you."

Before Andersson could utter another word, CIA agents along with Spanish law enforcement officers descended upon him, forcing him to the ground. Maddux asked one of the Spanish cops if he wanted to do the honors, and he readily obliged.

Andersson squirmed on the floor, a futile effort to regain his freedom. Even if he had managed to slip out of the handcuffs slapped on him, he would've struggled to leave the room given the amount of force and gun power surrounding him.

"Here's his MP," one of the agents said, holding up a Makarov pistol after fishing it from his pocket.

"Standard issue from the KGB," a Spanish officer chimed in.

Pritchett loomed over the Grand Prix driver. "My, my. Aren't we full of surprises."

"You are going to be full of regret before this is all over with," Andersson said.

"Perhaps," Pritchett said as he shrugged, "but it won't be on your account. Eliminating KGB vermin like you is what we do."

Standing toe-to-toe with Medved, Pritchett used his hook to stroke Andersson's face. "You're going to wish you'd stuck to simply driving cars."

"You're making a big mistake," Andersson said. "Whoever you think I am, you're wrong. I'm not KGB."

Pritchett nodded at the agents holding Andersson, signaling for them to carry away their prisoner.

Maddux approached Pritchett after Andersson had been secured in a car in the back alleyway.

"Do you believe him? You think there's a chance he isn't KGB?" Maddux asked.

Pritchett shook his head. "This is how the KGB trains their agents. Incessant denial until you start to question yourself and your training. Don't be so easily fooled."

"But what if he isn't? That would mean—"

"What? That the true Medved is still out there? Him and a handful of these other so-called super assassins still circling us like sharks? It's possible—or it's possible that this entire exercise was something the KGB did to see how gullible our agents would be. Either way, I have little doubt that Andersson is associated with some type of KGB operation. He even had a Makarov."

"I still think we need to proceed with caution. Nothing has changed the fact that we have a leak in our agency somewhere."

"And I still fully intend to plug it," Pritchett said. "I'll connect with you later, but we need to get moving. I have a spy to interrogate."

XI

PRITCHETT WASN'T FOND of working with other government entities. Navigating the territorial battles in his own country was challenging enough, but trying to maneuver among foreign law enforcement entities was next to impossible.

When Pritchett led the CIA's initial inquiry into working with the Spanish government on detaining a KGB assassin, he found officials to be open, offering to provide support rather than direct the operation. But once they reached the planning stages, not everyone was as cooperative.

Diego Diaz, the Spanish intelligence operative working with the CIA on the apprehension of Gunnar Andersson, initially proposed taking their prisoner to a station downtown. Spanish authorities reveled in any opportunity to gloat over trophy arrests, bringing the officers fame and serving as a warning to others conducting criminal activities. But Pritchett pushed back against the idea, explaining that they didn't want this to be publicized in case other opportunities arose out of the interrogation. Pritchett explained that Andersson might be amenable to a deal where he could serve as a double agent and help capture the other super assassins. Pritchett also reiterated his case by stating Andersson's arrest would mean little to the Spanish public. Eventually, Diaz came to a common understanding that the reasons for taking a prisoner to an environment where Spanish objectives could be met were worthless in this instance.

Pritchett also had another reason, which he didn't want to reveal—and that had to do with the CIA's interrogation tactics. All KGB agents endured enormous amounts of torture during their training to prepare them in the event that they were ever captured. The KGB's top brass warned that if any agent was ever captured, the option for a quick exit was always available with a poison pill. For that reason, apprehending Andersson was a delicate matter, requiring a swift takedown to ensure he didn't make a knee-jerk decision to end his own life. Though Pritchett realized that death might be preferable to the hell the CIA was about to put Andersson through.

The small adobe-style home nearly 100 kilometers outside of Barcelona on a remote ranch provided Pritchett with all the privacy necessary to get Andersson to talk. And they had plenty of topics to discuss.

Andersson's profile fit the mold for the type of civilian recruit the KGB preferred. That information was the launching point for Pritchett's interrogation.

When Pritchett entered the windowless room in the center of the house, he found Andersson handcuffed and chained to the chair. Sweat had already beaded up on his brow, the first trickle streaking down his nose and dripping onto the table in front of him.

"Could I please have a drink of water?" Andersson asked.

Pritchett poured a small glass and then held it up to the prisoner's mouth so he could drink.

"You know you've arrested the wrong man," Andersson said. "I don't know who you think I am, but I can assure you that I am not him. This is all a big misunderstanding."

Pritchett tossed the file on the table and smiled as he shook his head. "You really expect me to believe what you're saying?"

"It is the truth."

"Let's start with some facts about your life. You were born in Sweden and eventually moved to Germany to study engineering at the University of Stuttgart. Meanwhile, you dabbled in racing there during you free time and became a competent driver. Once you graduated, you decided to turn your hobby into your career and quickly rose through the ranks of several low-level racing circuits. But here's where things get interesting. Heidelberg Racing offered to sponsor you and then suddenly you move to the Soviet Union, where you supposedly lived for three years when you weren't circling a track."

"That is all true—and yet not a single criminal offense was committed," Andersson said. "Yet here I am, bound in chains."

Pritchett wagged his finger. "As always, there is more to the story, for Heidelberg Racing is operated by several men with Soviet sympathies. When you start to put all that together, along with the fact that we have intelligence reports of you training at a facility used by the

KGB to prepare agents, it adds up to the startling truth about one of open-wheel racing's up and coming stars: Gunnar Andersson is a spy for the KGB."

"That's a lie, and you know it," Andersson said with a growl.

"What I do know is that a message was delivered to you with my exact whereabouts, a message that adhered to the KGB's delivery methods for agents receiving a new target. And you showed up carrying a KGB-issued Makarov. Now, pardon me if I jump to any conclusions too quickly, but it's not a stretch of anyone's imagination that you were there on what you believed to be your new orders. And you were going to kill me."

"That can't be any further from the truth," Andersson said. "I was there to warn you that your life was in danger."

"Cute story, kid," Pritchett said. "But I'm not buying it. Your explanation falls apart when held up to the light of the facts."

Andersson looked down. "If you must know the full truth, it's that I am a double agent for West Germany, planted within the KGB to steal secrets and sabotage various operations."

Pritchett narrowed his eyes. "That's an even more convenient story, no doubt concocted to help you escape a situation like this."

"The CIA has double agents, no?"

"I will not allow you to use this interrogation to glean information out of me for you to report back to your superiors in Moscow."

Andersson shrugged. "I already know the truth as I have met a double agent already working for the CIA and the KGB. Where his true loyalties lie is a mystery to me, but what I am doing is not unique within the espionage community."

"I will not sit here and listen to any of these lies any longer," Pritchett said as he stood. He slammed his fist down on the table. "If you won't tell me the truth willingly, I'll have to get it out of you by other means." Pritchett slid a picture of Andersson's brother across the table. "Recognize this guy?"

Andersson narrowed his eyes and looked up at Pritchett. "You leave him out of this. I already told you the truth. He's just a kid."

"A kid we have in custody right now. He got picked up in Stockholm for theft and is facing a heavy sentence for his crime."

"Leave him alone," Andersson said as he twisted and turned. "I swear I'm telling you the truth. Call one of your friends in West Germany intelligence; they will confirm what I am saying."

Pritchett put his hook at the base of Andersson's chin. "I'm not playing around. Your brother will go to prison if you don't start talking."

"What else do you want me to say?" Andersson asked, pleading with his eyes. "I've told who I really work for. There's nothing more for me to say."

Pritchett backed away and paced around the room. He considered all his options, including the one where he could begin shocking Andersson. But he seemed up for the challenge physically. Even more discouraging to Pritchett was the fact that the racecar driver appeared convinced that the story he was telling was truth. As Pritchett mulled his next move, Diaz entered the room.

"We need to release him," Diaz said.

"Release him? What on earth for?" Pritchett asked.

"We checked out his story with some of our contacts in West German intelligence. Turns out he's telling the truth. He's a double agent."

Pritchett sighed. "Before we do that, I'd like to verify that myself."

"You can do that on your own time," Diaz said. "We need to release him now and clear this unit. Another criminal connected to a high-profile bank robbery case has been captured, and we need to convince him to help us set a trap for the ringleader."

"This is unacceptable. I need more time."

"Sorry, but your time is up. The Spanish government was gracious enough to allow you to conduct this operation on our soil, but you must play by our rules. And we say this man must be released and allowed to return to his normal activities before he gets exposed. He has one hour before he's supposed to make a scheduled check-in. And if he doesn't show up, there could be some costly implications for him."

"Thank you," Andersson said. "Finally someone around here who's the voice of reason."

Pritchett continued his protest. "The implications for CIA agents all across Europe could be far more costly if he's allowed to go free. I'm not convinced that his story is true, not to mention I don't fully trust you, Lieutenant Diaz."

"I'm not here to win your trust," Diaz countered. "I'm here to carry out orders. Now, I suggest you leave before I have you forcibly removed."

"Fine," Pritchett said as he scooped his file folder

off the chair. "I'll remember this and know who to thank the next time one of our agents returns home in a coffin."

Pritchett stormed out of the room, slamming the door behind him. He hopped into a car and asked the driver to take him to his hotel.

* * *

MADDUX CHECKED HIS WATCH and drained everything in his coffee mug but the dregs. He hadn't heard from Pritchett since he left with Andersson for the interrogation. In an effort to protect the CIA agents in unfamiliar territory, Maddux and Pritchett and the other two agents who had joined them all stayed in different hotels. The idea was that if they were being tracked by the KGB, the level of difficulty for killing all of them was raised exponentially.

Maddux phoned the hotel where Pritchett was staying and asked to ring his room. The phone rang a dozen times without an answer before the receptionist returned to the line.

"Would you like to leave a message?" she asked.

"I think I'm just going to head over there," Maddux said. "Have you happened to see Mr. Pritchett this morning."

"What does he look like?"

"Elderly guy, always wears a hat and a suit. He has a hook for an arm and a patch over one eye. He's hard to miss."

"I don't believe I've seen anyone matching that description since I started my shift two hours ago. But sometimes I don't notice people when I'm helping other customers at my desk or talking on the phone. He very well could've walked right past me and I didn't really see him."

"Maybe he just unplugged his phone for some reason. I'll try to reach him by knocking on his door," Maddux said before he hung up and headed straight for Pritchett's hotel.

The lobby of the hotel was relatively quiet. A man in the corner sat smoking a pipe and reading the morning edition of *La Vanguardia*. Two bellhops conversed quietly, while an elderly woman wearing sunglasses stood at the counter checking out.

Maddux knew where Pritchett's room was. Second floor, 205. Instead of wasting time checking in with the attendant at the front desk, Maddux went straight upstairs. He hustled down the hallway near the west end of the building toward Prichett's place.

But when Maddux arrived, he noticed the door was cracked. He pushed it open slowly and called out for his boss.

"You in here, Pritchett?" Maddux said.

No response.

"Pritchett, it's Maddux. Are you in the bathroom?"

He could hear the water running and didn't want to intrude on the old man's privacy.

"I'll be waiting in the lobby," Maddux said. "Just thought you'd want to know that your door was cracked. I'm going to—"

Maddux stopped in the middle of his sentence, his attention arrested by splattering of water against the tiled floor. He rushed over to the door and rapped against it.

Still no response.

"Pritchett, are you there?" Maddux asked again.

This time, Maddux turned the knob and pushed open the door. A growing puddle of water lapped at his feet and stretched across the floor. He looked up to see an empty tub. Rushing over to turn the water off, Maddux searched the area for any other clues as to what might have happened.

He rifled through the room and found Pritchett's personal effects, all neatly arranged in his suitcase, except for a stray jacket hanging haphazardly over the back of a chair and a pair of socks at the foot of the bed.

"Damn it," Maddux muttered.

Charles Pritchett was nowhere to be found.

XII

MADDUX WASTED NO TIME in phoning Diego Diaz to alert him to Pritchett's disappearance. The call wasn't received warmly, nor the request to invest manpower in searching for the Bonn station chief.

"I understand you have plenty going on, but you know how serious this is," Maddux pleaded. "Every minute we stay on the phone talking about this instead of searching for him is another minute head start for his abductors. And let's be frank about this, the KGB did this."

Diaz grunted. "We will do what we can. I'll send over two officers to investigate, but I'm afraid there's not much more we can do."

"What exactly happened last night with Andersson?" Maddux asked.

"Pritchett didn't tell you?"

"I didn't speak with him last night. I was out late, taking in a soccer match. Now, where's Andersson?"

"We released him."

Maddux's jaw fell agape. "You *what?*"

"We couldn't hold him based on the results of our investigation."

"*Your* investigation? We set up this trap to catch Andersson because we know who he really is."

"Your intelligence was wrong. He's not this Medved character you're looking for. Andersson is a double agent for West Germany."

Maddux was glad he wasn't standing next to Diaz because a swift punch to the gut would've been in order. "You're calling our intel faulty?"

"I follow the evidence, Mr. Maddux, and it led me to conclude that Andersson was telling the truth. He would've had to either have fooled the West Germans or had someone in intelligence there lie for him if anyone ever made any inquiries into his status. I think a reasonable man such as yourself can see that the chances of that are very, very low, inconceivable really. So, not wanting to start an international incident and blow Andersson's cover, I released him."

"And just like *that,* Charles Pritchett is missing," Maddux said as he snapped his fingers.

"Have you taken a moment to consider that perhaps someone else may have wanted to kidnap Charles Pritchett?" Diaz asked. "I've been in this business long enough to know that making enemies is far easier than making friends."

Maddux knew Diaz was right. It wasn't out of the question that Pritchett's abductors could have been from somewhere else. Another country, another spy, the mole within the CIA. But with Pritchett's kidnapping coming on the heels of Andersson's release just seemed too logical. Maddux wanted to keep an open mind yet found it a struggle. The blinders he had been wearing for the past few weeks while participating in the CIA's operation to catch Andersson kept him from considering other possibilities.

The two detectives Diaz dispatched handled Pritchett's disappearance like a routine case, far from the urgency Maddux felt the situation demanded. If Maddux was right about who was behind everything, the Spanish authorities would be to blame for creating an environment for such an event to occur.

Maddux returned to his hotel and waited by the phone for any news. After not hearing anything by late afternoon, he called the detectives to find out what else they had learned. They shared how they canvassed the entire hotel, showing Pritchett's picture to guests, and nobody even recalled seeing Pritchett the entire time during their stay. He had operated like a ghost, according to CIA protocol.

Maddux stewed over the fact that they showed Pritchett's picture around. The description of a guy with a hook for a hand and an eye patch should've been sufficient. Over the last year since Maddux had been in Europe, he hadn't seen a single person matching that description other than Pritchett. Maddux urged the men to keep this story out of the papers and out of the news, especially Pritchett's picture.

"Letting the public know is the best way for us to generate leads," one of the detectives explained. "Having someone's memory jogged about where they were when they saw something suspicious often produces the tip we need to catch the criminal."

"This isn't a criminal case—this is an intelligence matter. We need Pritchett found discreetly. I'm sure you can understand the reason why that is."

"We will do our best to accommodate your requests," the detective said before he hung up.

Maddux went downstairs and ordered a bottle of tequila. There wasn't much for him to do but sit and wait. And tequila sounded like a fine way to pass the hours.

When the bar announced its last call for the night, Maddux looked at his watch. Five minutes until midnight. He threw back the rest of his drink and headed upstairs. He only removed his shoes before he crashed on the bed.

The next morning, he awoke to a ringing phone. The grogginess he felt vanished in the anticipation of receiving good news from the Spanish authorities.

"This is Maddux," he said as he answered.

"I'm afraid we do not have any news for you," the detective said. "We have searched the entire area and have yet to see any signs that would point to an abduction of any kind."

"So, what are you trying to say? That Pritchett left on his own accord?"

"Yes, we believe that's what happened. And since you insist on keeping this alleged kidnapping—"

"It's not alleged—it happened."

"Okay, since you insist on keeping this kidnapping a secret, we don't have a way to confirm what we have found. So, unless you want to let us share his picture with the newspapers, I'm afraid we'll have to wait and rely upon a tip to come in from one of the hotel residents or else close the case. But based on what we've noted, we think Mr. Pritchett left on his own, albeit hurriedly."

"But why would Pritchett do that, especially without contacting us or leaving a note. That just seems so uncharacteristic of him."

"I find that when people get desperate, they do desperate things, things that don't always make sense to the rest of us who are not so panicked by our current situation."

"You can keep telling yourself that," Maddux began, "but I'm sure you know deep down that he's gone, whisked away by the very KGB agent you had in custody less than forty-eight hours ago."

"We will be in touch," the detective said.

Maddux growled and slammed the phone down on the receiver. He'd grown accustomed to the autonomy provided by the CIA. All the permission asking and strict guidelines created an unbearable burden when it came to accomplishing a mission. Yet, Maddux had been thrust back into what felt like the Stone Age, an era of plodding police procedure to solve a crime. Meanwhile, he knew that Pritchett was long gone and likely wasn't even in the country anymore.

Maddux sat on the foot of his bed and sighed. He closed his eyes and leaned back, trying to concoct a scheme for how to retrieve Pritchett. The jangling of the phone broke Maddux's concentration.

"Hello, this is Maddux," he said as he answered.

"Ed Maddux?" asked the man on the other line.

"You've got him."

"This is Al Bearden. We need to talk."

Maddux swallowed hard. Bearden was the CIA's senior officer in charge of all operations in Europe and Russia. He served on the agency's special counsel and was a confidante of the president, according to what Pritchett had said when Maddux initially joined.

"I appreciate you calling me, sir," Maddux said. "We've run into quite the political buzz saw here with the Spanish."

"I want you on the first flight back to Bonn, and we'll talk about this in person."

"But, sir, what about Pritchett? I'm still waiting to hear back from the local authorities about his situation."

"They can keep us apprised of the situation over the phone. Besides, I think you and I both know Charles Pritchett isn't anywhere near Barcelona now."

"I understand. I'll get there as soon as I can."

"Let me know when your flight will arrive," Bearden said. "I'll have someone pick you up from the airport and bring you directly to the station here. We have much to discuss."

* * *

MADDUX HAD HEARD rumors about Al Bearden but had never had a chance to confirm any of them until he returned to the Bonn station office. Several agents had mentioned how Bearden was the shortest man in the agency, standing at just five-foot-five. He also had a scar on his neck, which allegedly came from a fight he got into with his ex-wife, who was serving time in a federal prison for treason after getting caught selling secrets to the KGB. Other rumors claimed that he faked his baritone voice in an attempt to make up for his diminutive stature and that he once walked in on President Kennedy and Marilyn Monroe.

Maddux hadn't met every person in the CIA, but Bearden was strikingly short. And Maddux had a hard time believing there was any man in the agency shorter than the guy occupying Pritchett's chair.

Bearden had a pencil tucked behind his ear and was staring at some papers when Maddux rapped on the door.

"Come in," Bearden said, barely glancing up from his papers.

"You wanted to see me, sir," Maddux said as he slipped inside and closed the door behind him.

"You must be Ed Maddux," Bearden said, sifting through several file folders until he fingered the one for the agent sitting across the desk.

"Civilian recruit who helped us stop a potential chemical attack at the World's Fair in New York," Bearden said as he scanned the file. "Also a legacy agent. And able to connect with government officials around the world through your position at Opel."

"That's all correct, sir," Maddux said, unsure if Bearden was just reading off facts or asking for verification.

Bearden scratched around the inside of his collar, revealing the famous scar. It was thick and stretched far beyond any visible area even after he pulled back his neckline. He looked up and caught Maddux staring.

"You probably heard that my traitorous wife gave this to me," Bearden said.

Maddux shrugged. "I've heard rumors, but I'm not one inclined to take everything I hear at face value."

"Well, you're smarter than you look then because those stories are all pure horseshit. The truth is far less dramatic. I got it when I tripped on a cow pattie and fell while running along a barbed-wire fence as a kid at my grandfather's ranch. Ascribing the injury to my ex-wife is far more imaginative, though I'm not sure who comes up with these things and spreads them through the agency as if everything rumored about my past is the gospel truth. Let me tell you one thing—better verify several times over before you believe a thing around here."

"I understand."

"To underscore my point, let's take you, for instance. According to Pritchett's files, I'm supposed to trust you completely. Apparently, you're the next wonder agent. And while what you did in New York is impressive, I would prefer to see things for myself and verify them before accepting Pritchett's word, even though I would trust the man with my life."

Maddux nodded. "That's understandable. What's happening right now to our agents over here is disconcerting and downright disruptive to the entire intelligence gathering process."

"I'm glad you're amenable to this, so let's get to it," Bearden said before pressing the record button on a tape player and pulling out a sheet of paper to take notes.

Maddux glanced behind him out of the window and into the main office area. He caught several agents staring at him before quickly looking away when he was near to making eye contact. In an instant, his feeling about the meeting with Bearden soured. Maddux sensed this wasn't going to be a friendly encounter.

He was still looking out the window when the blinds snapped shut. Maddux hadn't noticed Bearden get out of his desk to do something about the nosy agents peering at them through the glass. Bearden settled back into his seat before continuing.

"What can you tell me about what happened after the suspected agent was apprehended?"

Maddux furrowed his brow. "You're talking about Andersson, correct?"

"Was there someone else you were pursuing?"

"No, Andersson was the only one."

"Then tell me about what happened after you caught him."

"To be honest, I don't really know. I returned to my hotel and killed some time with a dinner and some drinks at the bar. Nothing too memorable."

"Why didn't you go along with Prichett?"

Maddux sighed. "I wasn't invited, though I doubt I would've wanted to tag along either. Torture isn't my thing."

"Then why in God's name did you join the CIA? Torture is how we get answers."

"And what kind of answers did you get out of Andersson? We probably wouldn't be in this predicament if we had used other methods to extract information out of him. Instead, we're looking at a trained KGB assassin—a super assassin, no less—who is running around unfettered and picking off our agents at will."

Bearden remained silent but narrowed his eyes. "I think torture *is* your thing, Maddux. Right now, what you're doing to me—it might as well be considered one of the more tormenting interviews of my life."

"You ask the questions, and I give the answers. Seems like this process is working out just fine."

"So you weren't at the interrogation when we were extracting information from the alleged KGB operative?"

"I was not."

"Let me ask you another question then. Did you recently go to Belgrade?"

"Yes," Maddux said. "It was a joint venture between my nine-to-five employer and the CIA, which saved the agency some serious coin by agreeing to share the costs."

Bearden scratched down a few notes. "While you were there, why did you break into the station office?"

"Break into the station office? What on earth are you talking about?"

"Don't play coy with me, Maddux. I'm going to give you one last chance to come clean."

Maddux watched as Bearden fingered the edge of a file folder with his right hand and decided to bet on a bluff.

"Come clean about what?" Maddux asked, feigning ignorance.

"This," Bearden said as he flipped the folder open and shoved a picture of Maddux sneaking into the office. "Does that help jog your memory?"

Maddux eyed Bearden closely, debating for a moment the course of least resistance. Questioning the photo and clinging to the lie was one option, while telling the truth was the other. Then there was a compromise between the two.

"Okay, I went to the office and nobody was there, so I broke in," Maddux confessed. "If I'd had a key or if the building was staffed when I went down there, I wouldn't have needed to break in."

"What exactly were you looking for?"

"Any more intelligence I could get about the

KGB's super assassin program as well as Medved. With our entire station under threat and being stalked by this killer, I wanted to find out whatever else I could dig up on the guy."

"And what did you find?"

Maddux didn't flinch. "Nothing, not a single extra piece of information about him and the program."

"Did that surprise you?"

"A little. I mean, I fully expected there to be other ancillary documents tucked away in a folder somewhere. I figured somebody found something else that would've made its way into the file the agency was building on this program. But nothing."

"Maybe you were looking in the wrong place."

"That's possible, but I was in Kensington's office. I presumed that if the files were going to be anywhere, they'd be under a lock and key there."

"Did you find anything else?"

"No," Maddux said, lying without hesitation. "It was a fruitless trip."

Bearden pushed another picture from his file folder across the desk. "What's that in your hand here?"

Maddux shrugged. "I'm not sure, maybe papers I carried with me from my work. In case I got caught, I wanted to have a credible alibi."

Bearden eased back in his chair, templing his fingers and pressing them lightly against his lips. He took a deep breath and exhaled slowly before continuing. "Are you aware of how this looks, especially right now with all that's going on?"

Maddux nodded. "I admit my actions might make you hold me suspect, but I can assure you that the only thing I was looking for was more information—and I found nothing else on the KGB assassin program."

"Watch yourself, Maddux. There are security levels for a reason. You wouldn't want to find something you're not supposed to. Trust me when I say this, the less you know about everything else going on in the agency, the better. Focus on your particular case and nothing else. Don't go snooping around either and making yourself look guilty. Episodes like this could certainly be detrimental to your future here."

"I understand," Maddux said, nodding slowly. He felt like a schoolboy getting scolded by a headmaster for mischievous activity. It may have well been deserved, but that didn't lessen the edge of Bearden's sharp rebuke.

"According to what I've heard about you, Maddux, I expect better."

"I won't disappoint you again, sir," Maddux said, unsure if he could keep his promise. Bearden seemed like the kind of leader who could find fault with anything one of his subordinates did.

"You're dismissed," Bearden said, looking back down at the stack of papers piled on the desk. He grabbed one off the top and continued reading.

Maddux used the arms on the chair and pushed himself to his feet. Bearden had already moved on, both mentally and physically. As his eyes drifted back and forth across the page, he mumbled the words to himself.

Maddux slipped into the hallway and shut the door behind him. A new wrinkle had been thrust into his quest to find his father.

You need to be more careful next time.

The inner voice dishing out timeless wisdom in his

head was poignant as always.

* * *

ONCE MADDUX LEFT the office, Bearden glanced up to make sure the man he'd just spent the past quarter hour grilling was looking elsewhere. Bearden dialed the number of Malcolm Pointdexter. Less than a minute later, he was standing in front of Bearden.

"What is it, sir?" Poindexter asked.

"Do you know Ed Maddux?"

He nodded but remained silent.

"I'm going to give you a new assignment," Bearden said. "I want you to work on a surveillance case for me. For the next couple of days, keep an eye on Maddux, who's working on catching the KGB agent responsible for the disappearance of a couple of our people from the Belgrade station as well as Pritchett. Let me know immediately if you see him conducting any suspicious activity. Is that clear?"

"Yes, sir," Poindexter said. "I won't let you down."

Bearden was getting tired of hearing that line. He knew that inevitably someone would let him down. And if it was Maddux, Bearden would make sure that the civilian agent would regret it for the rest of his life.

THE NEXT MORNING, Maddux wrote up a report on the viability of using Barcelona's Grand Prix track for a commercial. During lunch, he made a visit to the Bonn station to find out if there had been any developments in the search for Pritchett. He decided to begin in the basement with Rose.

"Sounds like Barcelona was tougher than you anticipated," she said the moment he walked in the door.

"All business today, I see," Maddux countered.

"Pritchett is in trouble and needs our help. I don't think we have the time to stand around shooting the breeze and hearing about your long strolls on the beach and around that gorgeous city."

"You won't be missing anything as my account would bore you to tears."

"Then let's discuss our most pressing matter then."

Maddux nodded. "Has anything developed in the search for Pritchett?"

"As a matter of fact, something has. Do you remember seeing the shoe bug I was working on last year?"

He nodded. "You just needed a way to slip it into someone's shoe without getting noticed."

"Yes, well, that would've been a fool's errand in most cases. I was having trouble setting the bug, plus we had a little issue of battery life. But I came up with a viable solution. And it was simple: recruit someone with access to Milos Markovi , the head of the Yugoslavian secret police."

"His housekeeper?"

"Bingo. She was under a tremendous amount of stress due to her husband's large gambling debt and being the only person in her family with consistent work. I figured she might be agreeable to a deal that helped eliminate the debt and put extra change in her pocket."

"So, what does she do?"

"We first got her to give us Markovi 's shoes he wears to work every day. Every two weeks, we have her swap out the shoes with another pair that has a working battery and can transmit to one of our listening posts."

"And one of those posts had something to report about Pritchett's whereabouts?

She nodded. "Pritchett is being held at the Pejic House outside of Podkoren in the Upper Sava Valley, just across the border from Italy. It's where the SDB takes prisoners for initial questioning, and the KGB utilizes the facility sometimes as well. He won't be there longer than a couple more days, so we need to act quickly on this."

"I'll let Bearden know straight away," Maddux said.

"I already told him," she said. "And I think he's going to send you and another agent to Podkoren to go after Pritchett. But I could be wrong. I just thought I heard him say that to someone else as I was leaving his office."

"I'd be happy to get out of here for a few days. He was crawling all over me yesterday, quizzing me about what happened in Barcelona."

"Did anything else happen I should know about?"

He nodded and glanced over his shoulder to make sure the room was devoid of any other tech agents who might have prying ears. Once he was satisfied that it was clean, he continued in a soft-spoken voice.

"When I was in Belgrade, I broke into the station and found a file in Kensington's office with my father's legend scrawled on the tab—John Hambrick. Inside, I found a photo of Kensington with my father. I also found a piece of paper with an address on it in Barcelona, so I decided to check it out when I had some time to kill."

"It's a good thing you didn't get killed doing something stupid like that. You wouldn't want to walk into an unknown situation like that without at least some intel. The man there could've shot you on the spot."

"Well, I survived, but not before I met this strange man. The house might as well have been a fortress, and I would've had a difficult time getting in had it not been for the delivery man who was dropping off a package right around the time I arrived."

"Did you speak to the man living there?"

Maddux nodded. "He claimed he didn't know my father, but he seemed like he was hiding something."

"Maybe you're just thinking that because that's what you want to hear."

"I'm trying to keep an open mind about everything.

However, I grew more suspicious after speaking with the deliveryman, who said he didn't know the man's name because the packages are always addressed to someone different. I can assure you that things don't just seem strange because I'm wanting there to be a thread to tug on; that man was most definitely involved in some sort of nefarious activity. Whether or not he has any history with my father is unknown, but there was something going on there."

"Well, that investigation will have to wait," she said. "We need to get Pritchett back before it's too late."

MADDUX FINISHED HIS DUTIES at Opel before heading home just as dusk fell over the city. The street lamps flickered on as he strode down the sidewalk, joined by a throng of other workers who had just clocked out. The sounds were reduced to a collective thunder of footsteps and the occasional horn that blared at an inattentive driver or the screeching of brakes to avoid a collision. The conversations occurring between pedestrians were muted and sparse. This was the German way. Quiet and subdued—until it was time to gather at the nearest biergarten.

Maddux enjoyed the relative silence, which gave him time to ponder the events of the previous day or plan ahead for the next one. He had received the green light to travel to Yugoslavia from his boss at Opel with a bogus assignment of scouting a location for a potential future plant there. Such a directive gave him the leeway to roam about the country without fear of getting immediately arrested and imprisoned. At least if he got caught snooping about in areas where he shouldn't have been, there would be the hope of some type of due process. Maddux knew the whole situation was risky, but he had to go after Pritchett. The station chief had put his life on the line in an effort to catch Medved and, in doing so, became a bigger target.

"Beautiful night for a walk home," said a man in German as he sped past Maddux.

Maddux forced a smile and nodded, a momentary interruption to what occupied his thoughts. His transition from life in the U.S. to Germany hadn't been the smoothest, but he was reinvigorated by a new challenge within Opel and thrilled to get the opportunity to serve his country. However, he felt fortunate to have the opportunity to search for his father, even if the chance was afforded to him by the same organization that was keeping the full truth about his father's disappearance a secret.

As Maddux continued along his route, the number of fellow pedestrians dwindled to only a scant few. People peeled off into their apartment buildings and homes at a regular clip until Maddux was nearly alone. He had noticed one man on the opposite side of the street, who'd seemed to be taking the same path. The man wore glasses and a hat pulled down taut over his brow, keeping his identity shrouded beneath the pale lighting.

Maddux sensed that he was being followed and decided to implement his CIA training in the event that he needed to shake a tail. When Maddux reached the corner, he sat down on the bench for the bus and reached inside his jacket pocket. The pack of Lucky Strike cigarettes hadn't been opened since he bought them, occupying space as a prop for nearly a month along with his Zippo lighter. And now was the time to put them to good use. He put his head down to look at his smokes but glanced across the street to see what the man would do.

Flicking the lighter, Maddux ignited a cigarette and took a long drag from it. He glanced to his left and saw the man approaching down the street. Across from him, the man had stopped at the corner, acting as if he was searching for something in his briefcase.

That was all Maddux needed to see in order to verify his hunch. He stood, taking another drag while nonchalantly looking around for the nearest exit. He noticed an alleyway around the corner. All he had to do was wait for the bus to grind to a halt.

The brakes squeaked as the bus came to a stop at the corner, blocking him from the tail's view. Maddux hustled down the street, trusting that the bus would hold that position long enough for him to slip away.

Maddux eased into the alleyway and walked briskly along before approaching the sidewalk, a half a block away from where he'd just passed. He peered around the corner to make sure the street was devoid of the mystery man. Confident that it was clear, Maddux walked south along the street, in the opposite direction from his usual path. He decided to make a large loop before returning home.

As he began his updated route home, he passed several elderly ladies out walking their dogs and crossed the street where a handful of kids were engaged in a competitive soccer match. But everything felt normal again—as in no one was stalking him.

Maddux's mind drifted back to the assignment ahead of him in the morning and how he would rescue Pritchett. The help Bearden would provide would be important if not vital to the mission's success. In the brief time Maddux had spent with the CIA, he quickly realized that the missions were far more complicated than the ones he was assigned in the Army during the war. Collaboration was the key to success.

As Maddux turned these thoughts over in his head, he didn't see the large man leaning against the corner of an apartment next to an opening into an alley. The man grabbed Maddux by the coat and flung him up against the wall. Maddux winced as his back slammed into the bricks.

"We need to talk," the man said in a gruff voice.

Maddux's first inclination was to fight back, but he stopped as he eyed the man closely. He wasn't the same person who had been tailing Maddux earlier.

"What do you want?" Maddux asked, clenching both fists and bracing for a fight.

"You need to stop this nonsense of looking for your father," the man said. "It's going to get you and the people you love killed."

Maddux narrowed his eyes and considered a different tact. "If you know so much about my father, why don't you give me some answers? Maybe I'll comply with your request."

"All you need to know is that he doesn't want to be found. I think he's made that abundantly clear."

"Not to me."

"Can you take a moment to consider that maybe what he's doing right now needs to be devoid of outside interference, if you catch my drift?"

"The thought has occurred to me, but I'm not so sure he doesn't want me to find him. There are other possibilities I've also considered."

The man grabbed Maddux by his shirt and pressed him against the wall. "Well, here's one for you to sleep on. You're getting dangerously close to something you don't want any part of. And if you don't leave it alone, you're going to regret it. That much I can promise you."

The man released Maddux then punched him the gut and kicked him in the thigh, sending him sprawling to the ground.

"You might be able to lose that lousy tail you noticed, but you'll never see me coming," the man said before hustling into the alley.

Maddux groaned as he staggered to his feet. The little stunt designed to scare him away only made him more determined to find out what was really going on with his father.

XV

AL BEARDEN WENT DOWNSTAIRS for a smoke five minutes before midnight. He tapped out a cigarette and lit it before scanning the street for his appointment. Two minutes later, a man appeared around the corner.

"You're late," Bearden said. He blew a plume of smoke upward.

Malcolm Poindexter, who went by Dex within the agency, stood in front of Bearden, clad in a trench coat and a fedora. "I lost track of time while I was packing."

"I hope you didn't lose track of your assignment," Bearden said.

"He gave me the slip once, but I caught back up with him."

"How does that happen?" Bearden asked. "I swear, Dex, there are days I think you're the greatest field agent the CIA has ever seen. And then there are days I'm genuinely stunned that you can even feed and clothe yourself."

"Isn't that how it is for everybody?"

Bearden's cheeks sucked inward as his lips wrapped around the cigarette. He pulled it out and studied it before blowing smoke out of the corner of his mouth.

"That's a question for everybody else, not me," Bearden finally said. "What I really want to know is what happened tonight with Maddux. I'm assuming something went down or else you wouldn't have arranged this meeting."

"After he gave me the slip, I decided to backtrack because that's what I would've done if I had been in the same situation," Dex began. "So, I cut through one of the alleys and found him looping back around. I made sure he didn't see me again, but I happened to see him get accosted in the alleyway."

"A mugging?"

Dex shook his head. "No, it was something else. However, I'm not sure exactly who or what it was about."

"Surely you heard something."

"Yeah, but nothing that gave away any clues surrounding their meeting. Just a vague comment from a large man who warned that Maddux was getting dangerously close to something and he'd regret it if he kept it up."

"Those were his words? *Dangerously close?*"

"That's what it sounded like to me. I was standing around the corner, using a gutter pipe for cover, but I would swear that's the exact phrasing he used."

"Well, I knew he was up to something in Belgrade. Then he lied to me about it. Damn, I hate these civilian assets."

Dex shrugged. "Without these civilian assets, we'd be in a heap of trouble."

"Perhaps, but they don't think like a spy all the time. Sometimes I wonder how much worse off we'd really be without them."

"Well, they're never gonna go away, so you can file away that pipe dream. They're here to stay, and we need to learn to work with them and trust them."

"Who's side are you on anyway? His or mine?" Bearden demanded.

"I'm on my country's side, and I don't care to get pulled into a pissing war between you and one of our best assets. Is that clear enough for you?"

"Oh, Dex, today is definitely one of those days I hate you."

Dex grinned and patted Bearden on the back. "Well, tomorrow you'll love me, so there's that."

"That remains to be seen. Think you and ad man can bring back Pritchett safely?"

"I sure as hell hope so. You never know what you're going to get once you cross that Yugoslav border."

"Well, be safe and bring Pritchett back alive. We need him for the uphill battle we're facing with these KGB assassins running rampant all over Europe."

"Roger that," Dex said. "We'll do our best." He turned to leave.

"And Dex," Pritchett called.

Dex spun on his heel and spun around. "Yes?"

"Make sure you keep an eye on Maddux. I don't want him pulling one over on us."

"Tomorrow will be one of those days where you'll think I'm the greatest field agent you've ever seen. I promise."

Bearden grunted and flicked the cigarette into the street. "I hope you're right."

XVI

THE TRAIN RIDE to Venice went rather smoothly for Maddux and Dex. They picked up a car left for them by another agent and drove to the Yugoslavian border, a trip that was uneventful but bumpy. Rolling his window down, Maddux stuck his arm outside and felt the air rushing up against his hand as they puttered along.

"So, why did you decide to join the agency?" Dex asked.

"It just felt like the right thing to do. And you?" Maddux asked.

"I'm not gonna lie—I did it for the adventure, as well as anything to get out from underneath my parents' roof."

"That bad, huh?"

"The worst. My dad owns a butcher shop in New York City and expected his only son to take it over one day when he decided to retire. But there's no way in hell I want any part of that thing."

"That does seem like it'd become tedious work."

"That's one way to describe it. I prefer to just call it what it is—sheer torture. I swear if you ever saw how sausage was really made, you'd never even let it touch your plate."

Maddux put up his hand toward Dex. "Just let me remain ignorant, will you? If I had to give up sausage links, I don't know what I'd do."

"You'd eat a lot healthier, that's what you'd do."

There was a lapse in the conversation as they drove through rolling hills blanketed by vineyards.

Dex broke the silence. "So, what's this deal about your father and the CIA?"

Maddux furrowed his brow. "Who told you about that?"

"Everybody around here talks. For a bunch of spies who are supposed to be good at keeping secrets, they sure are lousy when it comes to interoffice gossip."

"What exactly are people saying?" Maddux asked, drumming his fingers on the steering wheel.

"Oh, you know, just how your father has been missing and how he disappeared—things like that."

"I don't really care to rehash everything about his disappearance. It's too painful. But I know he's alive somewhere, and I'm going to find him eventually."

"Is that another reason why you joined the agency?"

Maddux stroked his chin and nodded. "There are millions of reasons I could list as for why I joined, just millions. But I'm kind of with you as it pertains to what thrills me about this job. Our opportunity to see the world is something I never want to take for granted."

"But there are other reasons?" Dex asked, his eyebrows arched.

"Look, I don't know what you're digging for, but I

can assure you that all my reasons are above board—and, for the most part, pretty damn noble."

"Don't get so jumpy. I just like to know who I'm going into battle with." The next few minutes were filled with awkward silence before Dex broke it. "Let's start over, okay? I didn't mean anything by what I said."

Maddux gave him a sideways glance. "Just because we work in the world of espionage doesn't mean we have to hold everyone and everything in suspicion all the time. At some point, we have to trust each other."

"I agree. So let me start this conversation with a different type of question. Did you play any sports in school?"

"I was on crew. And you?"

"I hated sports, but I did earn a letter for debate team."

* * *

MADDUX'S POSITION WITH OPEL enabled him to move freely across the Yugoslavian border. He was still often put under watch by the SDB, but that usually depended on the purpose for his visit. When questioned by the border agent, Maddux explained that he was scouting out possible locations to build a plant. The lack of a more permanent destination during his visit brought heavy interrogation about all his planned activities while in the country, but Maddux was ready. In less than ten minutes, they had been waved through.

"I've never seen anything like that," Dex said. "This place is usually a nightmare to get into. I've been held up for several hours before."

"Maybe attempting to argue with someone isn't always the best tactic," Maddux said with a wink.

"Debate team skills have helped me convince many superiors to see things my way."

"Sometimes someone telling us *no* is a good thing. It makes us learn skills better suited for the real world where not everyone is going to fall for your manipulative tactics."

"Do you really think we entered the country scot free? If so, please explain to me the vehicle tailing us back there?"

Maddux glanced in his rearview mirror again. He had seen the car attempt to subtly follow them since they passed the border.

"I've been watching him. Just because I haven't lost him yet doesn't mean I won't. Sometimes you have to test a tail to make sure it's not a coincidence."

Less than a mile down the road, Maddux pulled into a service station to fill up on gas. The car zoomed past them.

"Still think he was tailing us?" Maddux asked.

"He'll catch up with us later," Dex shot back.

"Perhaps, but I'm going to head back about half a mile and take that road north. It'll get us to Podkoren without the SDB following us."

A half hour later, Maddux rolled into Podkoren and drove straight toward the prison located outside of town in the mountains. They devised a plan together to break out Pritchett before pulling in to a small hotel on the outskirts of town.

"*Zdravo*," the hotel clerk said as they approached the front desk.

"Hello," Maddux replied.

"Ah, you speak English. Welcome to Podkoren. Is

this your first time staying with us?"

Maddux nodded. "First time to Podkoren."

"In that case, let me tell you that you are in for a—how do you say it in Engish—ah, a treat. We have the best wine in the country."

"I'm not much of a wine drinker," Maddux said.

"You are missing out. We have a large wine cellar on the back of our property stocked with many varieties that have won awards all across Europe."

"Sorry, still not interested."

"All business, I see," the clerk said. "Very well then. Let me get you your keys."

Once they left the office and entered their room, Dex wasted no time in casting doom and gloom over Maddux's choice of accommodation.

"You know the clerk is going to call the SDB and report us, right? This entire country is brainwashed into helping the secret police. We should've just slept in our car."

"I'm not interested in fighting you on this—or every other decision that we have to make. If the SDB returns, we'll deal with like them like we did before. But I doubt that guy is going to call anyone on us. Did you see that tattoo on his wrist? He fought with the allies during the war. Not sure why or how, but I'd recognize the tattoo he had anywhere."

Dex shrugged. "I guess time will tell. Just be prepared is all I'll say about that."

Maddux tossed his bag on the bed closest to the bathroom. "I need to take a shower."

Maddux ripped open the stiff paper wrapping around the bar of soap and tried to lather up. The tepid water trickled from the faucet, extending the shower by several more minutes than it normally would've taken him.

Hot showers with strong water pressure—another reason to protect our freedoms.

After drying off, Maddux stepped into the room with only a towel wrapped around him. He noticed his bag was not lying in the same position it was before and a zipper was slid halfway open. He glanced over at Dex, who appeared to be reading a day-old version of the *Novosti* newspaper.

"Anything good in there?" Maddux asked.

Dex lowered the paper. "Just the same old propaganda bullshit. You'd think these people would wisen up after a while, but they seem incapable of believing anything but the Soviet's lies."

Maddux tried to assess whether or not his bag had been searched by Dex while listening to him rant about the Yugoslavian people's ignorance.

"I guess it'd be easy to conquer a nation full of lemmings, who are either unable or unwilling to fight back," Dex said as he continued his rant.

Maddux squinted and slowly moved closer to Dex after noticing something sticking out of his jacket pocket.

"What is it?" Dex asked.

Before Dex could get to his feet, Maddux lunged. Dex spun just enough to avoid a head-on collision and used his momentum to scramble around Maddux. But he managed to snatch the picture that had been sticking out of Dex's pocket. Maddux looked at the image and narrowed his eyes.

"What's wrong with you?" Dex asked before realizing exactly what Maddux had been after. "How'd you—"

Dex didn't have a chance to finish his thought before having to avoid an oncoming Maddux. The two grappled on the floor, trading positions of power. In the process of their fight, Maddux's towel fell off. Dex regained the upper hand, climbing on top of Maddux and forcing his head hard against the floor. Reacting quickly, Maddux grabbed his towel and forced it into Dex's face. Maddux broke free and spun behind Dex before putting him in a sleeper hold. A few seconds later, Dex went limp, collapsing to the floor.

Maddux glanced at the picture he'd taken from Dex. It was the one Maddux took from the Belgrade station of his father. Maddux hurriedly pulled on his underwear and pants before searching Dex's coat pocket for more evidence to confirm Maddux's suspicions. Inside was a familiar key. He studied it for a moment and then pulled his key ring out of his pocket, matching it with his house key.

Either he's the mole or he suspects me as the mole.

Both scenarios made Maddux uncomfortable. He figured that if Dex were the mole, he would be unpredictable and might sabotage the plan. Or if he thought Maddux was the mole, Dex might be under the orders to kill him. For all Maddux knew, the whole rescue plan could've merely been a ruse for Bearden to ferret out the person he suspected as the one passing secrets to the Soviets.

Maddux realized ultimately either outcome would jeopardize the mission, and he didn't have much time before Dex would regain consciousness. Working with urgency, Maddux snatched off the bed sheets, tossed Dex over his shoulders, and hustled toward the wine cellar.

The door to the wine cellar was locked, but Maddux laid Dex down and wasted no time in jimmying it open. Maddux scooped up his prisoner and hustled inside before pulling the door shut.

Flicking a lighter, Maddux held it up to see where he was going. A narrow staircase led farther underground until it opened up in cramped quarters, stocked with wine racks. In the back was a small door. Maddux opened it and found that it led to another storage area that contained a chair and a few dilapidated wine vats. As Maddux figured out the best way to secure his prisoner, Dex started to regain consciousness.

"Where am I?" he asked as he sat up.

Maddux punched Dex again and put him in the sleeper hold, buying some more time. Securing Dex took all of five minutes, but Maddux paused to admire his work. Dex was bound to the chair, and there was nothing in the room that he could use to cut through the sheet bindings. Maddux slid a piece of wood through the handle, making it impossible to open from the inside.

Not bad for a civilian asset.

Maddux hustled back up the stairs and to his room where he placed a call to Rose.

"Is everything okay?" she asked. "It's not like you to call me while in the middle of an assignment."

"To be honest, I need your help. Something has come up, and I need your expertise."

"Don't you have someone with you?"

"Yes, but he's not providing me the kind of help I need, if you know what I mean."

"It's nine hours away. Do you think I'll be able to make it before our old boss goes on the move?"

"All you can do is try to get here. I'll fill you in on the plan once you arrive."

Maddux sighed and sat on the foot of the bed. Combatting the KGB was challenging enough when he didn't have his own people to contend with. Dex may have been following orders from Bearden—or he could've been the leak. Either way, Maddux couldn't let it concern him.

The clock was ticking on Pritchett. It would only be a matter of time before the SDB moved him somewhere else. And if they did, the mission would change from difficult to impossible.

Maddux needed Rose there—and he needed her yesterday.

XVII

ROSE ARRIVED ALMOST TEN HOURS on the dot after Maddux ended their call. She didn't need much time to gather her belongings and equipment as she rushed to his aid. The drive had been tiring and one she feared would draw much suspicion, but her fake credentials posing as a nurse allowed her to get past border security without any questioning. Despite the fact that women had been spying for years, she knew it was easier for her to fly under the radar than her male counterparts.

After she pulled into the hotel parking lot, she grabbed her bag and found Maddux's room number. She tapped softly on the door.

Maddux peeked through the window before welcoming her.

"It's so good to see you," he said, gesturing for her to come inside.

"I got here as quickly as I could."

He glanced at his watch. "You made great time. How did you get here so fast?"

She nodded to her car, a Jaguar E-Type. "It helps to have a nice set of wheels."

Maddux shut the door behind her and took her bags. "Let's get you up to speed on what's going on."

She scanned the room. "Where's Dex?"

"That's what I need to get you up to speed about."

"What do you mean?"

Maddux sighed. "I don't trust Dex. He was acting strange during our ride over, and I found this in his pocket." He held up the photo and a key.

"What are those of?"

"This is a key to my apartment and a picture I took from the Belgrade station that Dex lifted from my belongings."

"He went through your stuff?"

"When we got here, I took a shower, but when I came out, I noticed something sticking out of his pocket. I yanked it loose, confirming what I suspected about him. Then I later searched him and found my apartment key. That added with the fact that he had been acting strange the whole trip over made me incredibly uncomfortable. And I don't want to attempt to break Pritchett out with someone I can't trust."

"Did you ask him about any of this?"

Maddux shook his head. "Not yet. I had to cool off first—and to be honest, I'm still hot about it."

"Perhaps there's a logical explanation for it all. We might want to talk to him first before jumping to conclusions."

"He said some things on the drive over that made me start to wonder about him already. I don't think I'm imagining anything."

"Maybe not, but I've found jumping to conclusions in this business can have devastating effects."

"It can also save your life," Maddux quipped.

"Why didn't you tell me about any of this before?" she asked.

"I couldn't risk having anyone hear us—either Bearden on your end or the SDB on mine."

She nodded, signaling that she understood. "So, where is Dex?"

"He's tied up in the wine cellar out back."

"And you're just going to leave him there? Someone may go in there and find him."

"I wanted to wait until you got here before I brought him inside. If he's going to talk, it will help to have you here."

"Well, what are you waiting on? Let's go get him."

Madux and Rose stepped outside into the cool early morning air. The sun had yet to rise in all its glory, but the mountains to the east of them were backlit from dawn's early glow. The motel employee who had welcomed Maddux caught him off guard.

"Hello, my friend," the man said. "Headed out early today?" He did a double take, glancing back at Rose. "You have a new friend? She's much prettier than your other companion."

Maddux forced a laugh. "No, it's not like that. She's just—"

"You don't need to explain anything to me," the man said, holding up his hands. "The room sleeps four. If your occupancy goes over that, we need to have a talk. Otherwise, enjoy your stay."

"Thank you," Maddux said. "You're also up rather early, aren't you?"

"I have to go fetch the wine for today. We like to

bring each day's supply in the morning when all is quiet and we aren't so busy."

Maddux tried to remain calm but was panicking inside. He hoped the man couldn't tell. Maddux's only hope was that Rose would follow his suggestive poke in the back.

"Your English is excellent," Rose said, stepping forward. "Where did you learn to speak it?"

"I need to get something from my room," Maddux said. "If you'll excuse me."

Rose continued to engage the hotel employee in conversation, while Maddux slipped back inside his room. He slid open the bathroom window and crawled through it and then hit the ground with a thud. After racing across the field behind the motel, he approached the cellar door and opened it. He flicked on his lighter and hustled down the steps and then into the room where Dex was still tied up and fast asleep.

Maddux shook him, and he squinted as his eyes adjusted to the dancing flame. Dex grunted and moaned, unable to speak due to the gag still stuffed in his mouth.

"You're coming back with me, but we have to hurry," Maddux said.

Dex tried to say something again, but Maddux couldn't understand nor did he have the time to do so. He picked up a board and smashed it on top of Dex's head, splintering the wood. Dex went limp and slumped over again.

Maddux hoisted up Dex and ascended the steps. After checking to see if the area was clear, Maddux hustled toward their room, praying that no one looked out the back and saw him. He stopped around the corner of the building to see if Rose was still talking with the man. Maddux breathed a sigh of relief when he saw that she was. He made eye contact with her, gesturing to her to end the conversation so he could sneak Dex into their room.

A few seconds later, she gave the motel employee a pair of kisses on the cheek before taking his arm. She led him in the opposite direction, away from Maddux and around the far end of the motel.

Maddux hustled toward his room when a door two rooms from theirs swung open. A portly gentleman toting a briefcase stepped into Maddux's path.

The man scowled and looked at Maddux caught in the awkward situation. Saying something in Serbian, the man shook his finger at Maddux.

Maddux didn't know how else to diffuse the situation due to the language barrier other than a pantomime scene.

"My friend here drank too much last night," Maddux said, pretending to throw back alcohol before staggering around. "He's very ill. Hopefully he learned his lesson."

The man nodded as if he understood. He smiled and patted Maddux on the shoulder before getting in the car.

Maddux hustled into their room and dropped Dex onto the bed. Scouring the room, Maddux used an extra set of bed sheets tucked away in the top of the hanging closet to bind Dex again. Maddux moved Dex to the floor and secured him to one of the legs on a sturdy oak desk.

Dex was regaining consciousness when Rose slipped into the room.

"You're amazing," Maddux said as he tightened the knots on the sheet.

She sat on the edge of the bed, her eyes widening as she watched Maddux work.

"That was interesting," she said. "It's not every day that a man you just met tries to proposition you in a wine cellar."

"He probably thought—"

"Don't say it. I know good and well what this looks like," she said, pointing back and forth between them. "I'm just doing my job. Well, sort of."

"I'm just glad you understood what I wanted you to do."

"You looked terrified," she said.

"It was that obvious?"

"We need to work on your poker face. You might be able to get by with a motel clerk in the shroud of near darkness. But other people you may come in contact with will be able to sense your angst."

"Okay, there will be time for that later, but right now, we need to put together a plan for breaking out Pritchett before the SDB moves him."

Maddux and Rose spent the next twenty minutes drawing up a strategy for how they could extract Pritchett without inciting a full-blown international incident.

"You think this will work?" Maddux asked when they were done.

"There's no such thing as foolproof, but I think this plan is as close as it gets—as long as the SDB doesn't decide to move him early."

"Sounds good. Do you have everything you need?"

"There are a couple of gadgets in my car that I

want to bring. Other than that, we should be good to go."

Maddux clapped his hands and rubbed them together. "Then let's get to it."

They both grabbed their bags and headed outside. Maddux lingered in the doorway and stared at Dex. After saying a short prayer for Dex to stay put, Maddux secured the door, unaware that Dex was wide awake.

XVIII

MALCOLM POINDEXTER wasn't convinced that Ed Maddux was the mole from the Bonn station, if there even was one. Despite the CIA's best efforts to shuttle secure messages between locations, the opportunity for prying eyes to fall upon classified documents was greater than the agency would've hoped. Publicly, the CIA boasted about its ability to transfer information to agents halfway around the world without anyone being able to crack their codes. But such a statement was far from the truth. Privately, the CIA adopted a method of "post and pray" when it came to delivering sensitive reports to distant destinations—send the message and pray it doesn't fall into the wrong hands.

But Dex wasn't allowed to make judgment calls when it came to working under Al Bearden. Serving under Bearden in the past at the CIA's Cairo station, Dex learned that doing anything other than what the chief wanted was detrimental to a thriving career. Dex felt more like a foot soldier carrying out orders than a trained asset capable of making sharp decisions on the fly and following the evidence. And bringing back Ed

Maddux was the only viable option, according to Bearden. The ultimatum was simple: get one piece of damning evidence on Maddux and bring him back to Bonn.

When Dex first began his trip to Podkoren, he wasn't sure he would get any proof that could be considered "damning." Ed Maddux seemed genuine and sincere in his dedication to the agency. His slip of Dex's tail could be forgiven and probably lauded as an alert spy. Dex had all but written off Maddux as the leak when he'd climbed into the shower.

But Dex wanted to make sure he'd done his due diligence. With Maddux in the shower, his bag was wide open. So Dex took a peek.

When the door to the bathroom swung open, he was looking that picture of Maddux's father taken from the Belgrade station. Dex hurriedly shoved it into his coat pocket, but not all the way. But that wasn't all Dex had on him.

In the inside coat pocket, he hid away a key to Maddux's apartment that Dex had been carrying since Bearden doled out the assignment. The key was be used in case the situation warranted it. So far, it hadn't. But Dex had forgotten that the key was still nestled inside.

As Dex struggled to free himself of all the bindings that kept both his mouth closed and his limbs virtually immobile, he put all the pieces together. Imagining the situation from Maddux's perspective, Dex saw how his colleague's already heightened suspicion of everyone along with being tailed and having his stuff rifled through while in the shower could lead to such a violent reaction. Dex wanted to explain, but he never had the opportunity.

However, Dex had faked being unconscious and learned of Maddux's plans with Rose to break Pritchett out. Dex viewed the plan as disastrous, destined to fail before it even got off the ground. If he didn't stop them, two bad things were likely to happen. First, Maddux and Rose would either be killed or captured. Secondly, the security around Pritchett would increase, making a rescue mission virtually impossible. Then there was the problem of how to handle this situation with Bearden. Dex needed to return them to Bearden and let him deal with the mess. It was the only potential to earn some goodwill out of the debacle. But Dex couldn't get ahead of himself; he still needed to apprehend the other two agents to keep matters from getting even worse.

Dex tried to scream, but the sheet stuffed in his mouth muted any such attempts. He scanned the room for anything that might help him break free of the bindings. Without enough leverage to lift the desk and slide the rope down the leg to get untied, he sought another option. Against the baseboard was a floor heater, shrouded in a metal casing. The unit had become worn and full of sharp edges on the corners.

That'll do.

Dex locked his feet underneath the bed and strained to drag the desk from one side of the room to the other. Slowly the hulking piece of furniture budged, inching across the floor until Dex reached the heater. The entire escape was an exercise in patience, realizing that in order to succeed, he couldn't rush anything. If he moved too vigorously while scooting the desk and himself across the room, he could wrench his back. And if he attempted to cut through the rope too quickly, he could fray the metal to the point where it would be too flimsy to slice through anything of substance.

The whole process took just under twenty minutes. Once Dex was free, he grabbed the keys to their car and went straight to the prison location, hoping that he wasn't too late.

Dex parked about a quarter of a mile away from where Maddux and Rose had planned to launch their operation. They were hidden along the top of a ridge shrouded with heavy trees and shrubs. But Dex knew they were there.

He passed Rose's car tucked behind some bushes off the side of the road. If he hadn't known it was there, Dex figured he would've missed it. That revelation made him slow down. Sneaking around in enemy territory was bad enough, but he also faced the daunting odds of being opposed by his colleagues. Dex had no allies, so he couldn't afford even the slightest misstep.

Easing within twenty meters of Maddux and Rose, Dex stealthily made his final approach and committed to the encounter. Maddux didn't turn around until Dex had already jammed his gun into the small of Maddux's back.

"Surprised to see me?" Dex asked softly in Maddux's ear. "You need to thank me because I'm saving your life."

"Pritchett is going to be gone for good if we don't get him out now."

"You *all* would've been gone for good if you went through with this plan. I heard everything while pretending to be knocked out. You're still plenty green, Maddux. And so is Rose when it comes to activity in the field."

"Our plan would've worked," Maddux said.

"Start walking toward your car," Dex said. "We'll talk about it on the way back to Bonn."

XIX

MADDUX WANTED TO LASH OUT at Dex once they arrived back at Rose's car but decided to keep quiet. Considering that Dex wanted to take them back to Bonn instead of killing them and burying them in a Yugoslavian forest was a sign to Maddux that maybe he had misread the situation. He also didn't want to agitate Dex to make matters worse for Rose. She offered her assistance innocently enough, yet Maddux knew his withholding all the facts might cost him some portion of the trust he had built up with her if he was wrong about Dex. Though Maddux considered that it might not matter in the end. His offense of shackling a fellow agent might be egregious enough for dismissal.

No one said a word until they reached the border.

"Don't worry," Dex said, digging into his back pocket. "I packed all your belongings and paid the motel bill. I've got your passports right here."

After they cleared the border, Dex started talking.

"I should give you a beating you wouldn't soon forget for that stunt back there," he said. "That was reckless and uncalled for, not to mention that it had the potential to get us both killed."

Maddux sighed. "I thought that—"

"I know what you thought, that I was either the mole or that I suspected you as the mole. The truth is, Bearden told me to keep an eye on you. You shook my tail in Bonn, but I hadn't drawn any conclusions. However, I must admit that you looked pretty damn guilty with the way you were being very evasive."

"So, that was you who was following me around that night. Care to explain the key you had to my apartment in your pocket?"

"I forgot I still had it on me. But that's standard operating procedure when you're tailing someone you suspect. Your station chief has a copy of a home key for every person on the CIA payroll under his purview. Spies are notoriously suspicious of everyone, even their own."

"You were going to enter my apartment and snoop around?"

"We're dealing with a mole here, and your story was sketchy. You knew where Pritchett was staying in Barcelona. If anyone could've ratted him out, it could've been you."

"Yet you don't seem convinced that I'm the mole now."

Dex shook his head. "You care about Pritchett too much, and it's evident to me. However, it's not my job to decide if you're sharing secrets with our enemies. My job was to follow you and report back what I found. The ultimate call about what happens to you will fall on Bearden. And when he gets set on something, he doesn't like to change his mind. For your sake, I hope Bearden agrees with the conclusion I've come to."

Maddux exhaled before punching the car door. "If that's how you felt about me, why didn't you let us stay and rescue Pritchett? He's going to disappear into the KGB's system, and we're never going to hear from him again."

"I wouldn't be so sure about that. We've got eyes and ears everywhere. Isn't that right, Rose?"

Rose stared out the window and remained quiet.

"Rose?"

"Yes," she said.

"Isn't that right?" Dex asked.

"Isn't what right?"

"Don't you have a program that has eyes and ears all throughout the KGB network?"

"I wouldn't say we have their organization blanketed, but we do have quite a few people listening. However, our coverage inside Yugoslavia is spotty at best."

Maddux turned around to look at her. "So what does that mean?"

"It means that we're not likely to hear anything about Pritchett's movement."

Maddux punched the dashboard. "I knew it. We're gonna lose him. And if anybody knows how to plug this leak and help us get back to the business of capturing these KGB assassins, it's Pritchett."

"Just calm down," Dex said. "This business of espionage is as unpredictable as it is frustrating at times."

"You're just saying that because you know you're responsible if Pritchett is swallowed up by the KGB. Who knows what they'll do to him to get the information they want?"

"If the KGB is smart, they'll keep him safe and sound so they can trade him for one of their spies that we've captured."

Rose leaned forward. "But there are no guarantees. You know that as well as anyone, don't you?"

Dex kept his gaze fixed on the road and didn't answer.

Maddux turned to look at Rose. "What happened?"

"Well, it's a long—" she began.

"Now's not the time, Rose," Dex said.

"Are you ever going to talk about it?" she asked. "At some point, you need to."

"Some day, but not now."

Maddux settled back into his seat and took in the scenery of the Alps as they sped back toward Bonn. He wasn't looking forward to his impending confrontation with Bearden.

* * *

THE NEXT MORNING, Maddux glared at Bearden upon entering the conference room at the CIA offices in Bonn. Rose and Dex settled into their seats and left the one directly in front of Bearden open for Maddux. He pulled the chair out and leaned forward.

"Every minute we sit here is more time lost searching for Pritchett," Maddux said, hammering the table with his index finger for emphasis. "Instead, we're all sitting around here in a worthless meeting."

Bearden interlocked his fingers behind his head and nodded subtly. "I understand you're upset, but please hear me out. With Pritchett gone, my job first and foremost is to figure out who's leaking information to the KGB because it's evident that somehow precious intel is getting outside these walls. And I don't intend to leave any stone unturned."

"If you think it's me, you're looking in the wrong direction."

Bearden grunted. "You've already lied to me once, so pardon me if I don't exactly see you as a beacon of trustworthiness right now."

"I already told you that I was looking to find out more information and find out about my father."

"Working for the CIA is a privilege, and it sure doesn't give you permission to go on some damned fool's errand in search of your father, rifling through top-secret files and then lying about it."

"Then stop the whispers and the secrets and tell me where he is and what really happened to him. It shouldn't be that difficult to share with an agent the truth about his father."

"Unfortunately, that's not my call to make," Bearden said. "If I could, I would. But that's not the situation we're in right now. And to be very frank, it's not the most important issue facing this station—or even you, for that matter."

"We also have a station chief whose life is in danger after being captured by the KGB, if he isn't dead already. If he were here, he'd—"

Bearden pointed at Maddux. "But Pritchett isn't here, and we need to focus on what we can do now to control the situation."

"Like dragging me back from Podkoren when we're on the cusp of extracting Pritchett?"

Bearden rubbed his face with both hands and

sighed. "You tied up your partner and begged Rose to join you there, endangering her life. And you think that I'm crazy for suspecting you and that I should've just done what? Left you out in the field to complete the crazy scheme you concocted to break Pritchett out?"

Maddux stared pensively at Bearden. "Look, I know I haven't been at the agency as long as all of you or anyone else in this room, but I sincerely think you're looking in the wrong place for the person leaking this classified information."

Bearden forced a smile and cocked his head to one side. "Why don't you share with the rest of us? I suppose you have a working theory."

Maddux nodded and scrunched his nose. "Sort of. But I need to speak with Pritchett first about it."

"That's not helpful. And what we need right now are ideas and theories to put a stop to these KGB assassins who uncannily seem to know where some of our most well-placed assets are located."

There was a knock on the door, and Bearden motioned for Pritchett's assistant to enter.

Maddux continued. "Sir, if you'll give me a chance to figure out a way to bring Pritchett home, maybe we can solve this more quickly than you thought possible."

"But our problem hasn't changed. We aren't going to be able to solve anything quickly because we don't know where Pritchett is right now."

Bearden's assistant raised her hand. "Uh, sir, if you will—I think we might actually know where Mr. Pritchett is being held."

"Go on."

She pushed her glasses up on her nose and looked

at the notepad in her hands. "We just received a message from one of our assets at a listening station in Yugoslavia. He captured information about moving a CIA agent last night. Based on where this intelligence came from, our analyst here believes it's Mr. Pritchett."

Everyone glanced at Bearden.

"Well, Maddux, looks like you might get to share your theory with us after all—that is if you can work together with Dex this time instead of tying him up and calling for reinforcements. Think you can handle that?"

"You won't be disappointed, sir," Maddux said.

"I better not be—because if you fail, I'm going to put you on a plane and send you back across the Atlantic. Do I make myself clear?"

Maddux nodded and stood. He needed to get moving if they were going to find Pritchett.

XX

MADDUX WAS LESS THAN THRILLED about making another long trip back to Yugoslavia, especially since he staunchly believed he never should've been dragged away in the first place. Had Dex been more accommodating, he could've waited until after Maddux and Rose extracted Pritchett from the SDB holding facility in Podkoren. But Maddux realized there was no use in pining about the past. Pritchett remained in the SDB's custody, and they weren't about to let him get away. At least, not without a savvy escape plan.

Maddux invited Dex to join him in the basement before they hit the road. Dex accepted, and they stepped onto the elevator together and descended into Rose's domain.

"Welcome, gentleman," she said as she paced back and forth in front of one of her worktables. "Well, there's some good news and some bad news."

"I'd rather hear the bad first," Dex said. "The good will soften the sting afterward."

"Too bad," she said. "You'll hear it in the order that I heard it. So, the good news is that we know where

Pritchett is—at least, we think we do. He has been taken to Konjic along the Neretva River. We have plenty of intel on that SDB prison since we've had several agents who've been held there."

"And the bad news?" Dex asked.

"The location is heavily guarded and extremely difficult to get in and out of without being seen," she said.

"It's not that bad," Dex said. "You guys down here always make everything sound so doom and gloom."

"Would you care to refute the report and share with us how the prison is all rainbows and roses with a paved road leading to the prison gate?"

Dex closed his eyes and shook his head slowly before responding. "Rose, Rose, Rose. When are you ever going to thoroughly read my file? I know you do it all the time. I've seen you scanning other agents' profiles as you decide what tech someone will need to make their mission easier."

"Perhaps all you need is a bobby pin and you can jimmy the lock, walk right in, grab Pritchett, and walk right out. Simple enough, right?"

"You're making it sound like it's as easy as going to the corner market for a six pack. It is heavily guarded, but there are ways in and out."

"Such as," boomed Bearden from the back of the room. He strode toward them, his footsteps echoing throughout the cavernous facility.

"A tunnel, maybe," Dex said. "Or scaling the fence when the guards aren't looking."

"Did you just say those ideas out loud, Dex?" Bearden asked.

Dex pursed his lips and tilted his head to one side.

"Okay, so maybe those aren't the most practical ideas given the fact that we need to get Pritchett out of there in a hurry."

Maddux chuckled.

"What is it?" Dex asked.

Maddux smiled. "I just pictured Pritchett using a spoon to shovel out dirt from his cell. It was quite comical—not to mention that it will never happen."

"Yes," Bearden said. "We need something better than that, something that will actually help him escape the SDB's clutches right away."

"You know a thing or two about that facility, don't you?" Rose asked , eyeing Bearden.

"More than I care to know."

"Have you been there?" Maddux asked.

"I got taken there several years ago when we had an operation go south in Belgrade," Bearden said. "Fortunately, the place wasn't as heavily guarded then as it is now."

"You escaped?" Dex asked.

Bearden nodded. "I put a guard in a sleeper hold, switched clothes with him, and walked right out of there. Took me less than a week to recognize the opportunity, and I went for it."

"But things have changed?" Rose asked.

"Based off the reports I've seen, they've made significant changes since I was there."

Dex glanced down at the documents in front of him. "From what I've read, this place is highly fortified. We're not getting inside this place, at least not without a few dead bodies scattered around."

"Or so it would appear," Bearden said.

"You have some other ideas?" Maddux asked.

"I think so. Given everything that's happened since I was held in Konjic, surprisingly there is one thing that hasn't changed."

"And what's that?" Dex asked.

"The man running the place, Goran Jankovic. He somehow survived the fallout from my escape, which I know the KGB was upset about. They didn't force the SDB to replace him as head of the prison, which is still puzzling. I'm not sure why that is, but I'm glad they didn't. I have an idea on how we can get inside and get Pritchett out without anyone noticing."

"What are we going to do, just walk right up to the gate and knock?" Dex asked with a chuckle.

"That's the idea," Beraden said. "Are you up for the challenge?"

XXI

PRITCHETT FELT HIS LEGS go numb after sitting chained to a metal bench in a transport truck for more than two hours. The only thing illuminating the back of the vehicle was a pair of thin slits near the top of the roof on each sidewall. With pale light trickling inside, Pritchett guessed it was either early morning or late evening, though he couldn't be sure. Since he was captured in Barcelona, he had endured hours of interrogation along with regular sleep deprivation. He lost his sense of time since being taken. He closed his eyes for just a moment only to get slapped in the face by a nearby guard.

"No sleep during transport," the man said, grabbing Pritchett by the chin and forcing his head against the wall.

Pritchett looked down at the bucket a few feet away that contained his hook along with his eye patch. He could only imagine how hideous he looked to the guard.

But Pritchett was more concerned with the mystery of how he was nabbed by a KGB operative. With the possibility that the mole could leak the plan, Pritchett made sure that the only people who knew about the mission were those involved. However, given his current situation, he could only assume that either one of the people who knew was the mole or that one of them wasn't careful with the details of the operation. The goal of apprehending Andersson succeeded, but not without a hefty price, one Pritchett was paying personally. Ultimately, the end result was a disaster. Andersson managed to elude further detainment thanks to the Spanish authorities, and the KGB caught the Bonn station chief.

When the overhead light flickered on, Pritchett saw his reflection in the stainless steel wall opposite of him. Though not the sharpest image, he could tell his face was covered with stubble, his hair disheveled. He concluded that solitary confinement would be a dream as he would be content to be placed anywhere alone. No more flashing lights. No more yelling and screaming. No more threats. Just a dark box and silence. Seconds after stepping out of the truck, Pritchett realized that was never going to happen.

Two men snatched him before he could take more than a few steps, whisking him away to an interrogation chamber. They secured Pritchett in a chair, cinching his arms down with leather straps. He smiled as the guards were befuddled over how to handle the extra wrist belt. Pritchett shrugged when they looked at him as they tried to decide what to do. They eventually chose to just leave it alone before exiting the room.

A single light bulb hung above him, swaying gently when the door swung open.

"Mr. Charles Pritchett," said the man striding into the room. He spoke in English with a heavy eastern European accent. "I've been looking forward to speaking with you for quite some time now."

"Perhaps if the circumstances were different, I might feel the same way," Pritchett said. "Who you are again?"

The man chuckled. "I supposed introductions are in order since we've never met. Though I won't be able to shake your hand like a proper gentleman."

"I don't think we need to pretend that we're proper gentleman, do we? I think we both know we're far beyond pretending to be anything other than what we are."

"And what are we, Mr.—?"

"Goran Jankovic," he said. "And we are spies. There is very little that is gentlemanly about what we do."

Pritchett shrugged. "Maybe that's just you. I always try to conduct myself as a gentleman. I've found it serves me well, even in situations like this."

"So, this isn't your first time being tethered to a chair and interrogated, no?"

"I've survived my share of interrogations, though not always as intact as when I entered."

Jankovic glanced down at Pritchett's hand. "I bet they still didn't get what they wanted, did they?"

Pritchett shook his head. "And neither will you, which is why you should let me go so we can discuss things like gentlemen instead of savages."

"Are you suggesting that I am a savage?"

"No, but I have seen perfectly reasonable men turn into them after not getting what they wanted."

"And why do you think I won't get what I want out of you?" Jankovic asked.

"I'm not certain about anything in this business. Guess it depends on what you're looking for."

"We're looking for John Hambrick and thought you might know where he's hiding."

Pritchett's eyes widened, and he shook his head. "John Hambrick—now that's a name I haven't heard in quite some time."

"That doesn't answer the question."

"I didn't know you had asked one."

Jankovic looked down at the bucket containing Pritchett's hook and eye patch. Grabbing the patch, Jankovic hustled over to Pritchett and put it in place.

"I can't stand to look at you for a second longer with that eye. What happened?"

"I don't want to talk about it."

"You don't want to talk about much of anything, do you?" Jankovic said with a sneer. "Fortunately, this chair is designed to make people tell secrets they swear they won't tell."

Pritchett watched Jankovic untie a bundled-up tool set and begin to sift through it.

"I don't know where John Hambrick is."

"Likely answer," Jankovic said, pausing from arranging the tools as he glanced at Pritchett. "It might be a while before I'm completely satisfied with it."

"Pulling my teeth won't help me magically conjure up Hambrick's location. I haven't heard from him in quite a while. And from what I last heard, we're not sure what side he's truly working for."

"Do you think I'm that big of a fool?" Jankovic asked as he inspected the blade of a scaffold. "We definitely don't believe the Americans woke up one morning with a solution for how to successfully launch a satellite into space. Someone gave you our secrets."

"And John Hambrick is the only person who could've sold your secrets to us?" Pritchett asked, huffing a laugh through his nose. "And yet you think I'm the delusional one. What a pity."

"Do not mock me. We both know the truth, only you're not quite willing to admit it. But don't worry. By the time I'm finished with you, you will tell me anything I want to know just to make the pain stop. Now open up and say ah."

Pritchett remained tightlipped, refusing to banter with Jankovic. Pritchett's fear of getting something shoved into his mouth trumped his desire to fire back. Watching the blade get nearer made him contemplate fabricating a story, anything to prevent the inevitable pain.

A knock at the door interrupted Jankovic's assault. He turned and looked over his shoulder.

"Come in," he shouted in Serbian.

A guard hustled across the room and whispered something in Jankovic's ear before exiting the room.

Jankovic replaced his tools on the table and took off his gloves. "We will continue this later. I have some more pressing business to attend to. Don't go anywhere."

Pritchett glared at Jankovic and tugged on the leather straps. They didn't budge.

A pair of guards entered the room and looked at Pritchett closely for a moment before glancing down at the bucket near the table.

"Looking for this?" one of the men asked before breaking into laughter.

"I wouldn't play with that thing if I were you," Pritchett said. "You might live to regret it."

The guard waved dismissively at him before working to untie Pritchett. They picked him up and ushered him toward the door, but Pritchett wasn't in the mood to make things easy on them. Instead, he fell limp and the two men were forced to drag him down the hallway to his cell.

With a violent heave, they shoved Pritchett inside and he stumbled as he went, stopping by skidding across the dirty cobblestone floor. He watched as the door clanged shut and heard the two guards laughing as they walked down the hallway.

He didn't know how much time he would have before his next encounter with Jankovic, but Pritchett could only hope it was long enough to come up with a plausible story that would keep him alive for an attempted escape or an extraction. No matter what, he needed to get out as soon as possible.

XXII

MADDUX ADJUSTED HIS TIE and smoothed back his hair around his ears. The long road trip from Bonn had left his clothes slightly wrinkled and rendered his hair unkempt. Looking sharp was critical to the new operation. He grabbed the crate from his trunk, hoisting out the bottles before setting it gently onto the ground. With a final scan of the area, he put his hands on his hips and looked at Dex.

"You think this will work?" Maddux asked.

"First time adopting an alias?" Dex responded.

"No, but I've never assumed one this far behind enemy lines."

Dex knelt down and tied his shoes. "You'll be fine. Just keep it simple and stay calm. If Jankovic is into this stuff half as much as Bearden said he is, we should just be able to walk in there and take Pritchett."

"But didn't you say things never go as planned?"

Dex chuckled. "I didn't coin that phrase, but it certainly can apply to anything we do, especially on a mission like this."

"Well, for my day job, I do try to sell cars to people."

"That's hardly your day job any more, in case you haven't noticed. I'll predict in six weeks, your time spent at Opel will be merely window dressing for the KGB agents sniffing around."

Maddux shrugged. "Maybe, but I like my job there."

"Yeah, but you like this job more. Besides, it suits you better."

"You think so?"

"Look, you're relatively new to all of this espionage business, yet you managed to shake my tail the other day. That doesn't happen to me. You're the one who is just getting started here, yet you pulled off something very few people have been able to do when I've been following them. It may not mean much in the grand scheme of things, but it means you've got a natural knack for this business. You also have some passion for it, too. And that's rare to see these days."

"If I'm being completely honest here, my passion is fueled mostly by my quest to find my father," Maddux said. "I appreciate the kind words, but I'm not sure this is what I want to be doing twenty years from now."

"In this business, just to be alive twenty years from now is a goal worth setting. And it means you're doing something right."

Maddux looked down at the crate before snatching it up and lugging it along as they walked toward the gate.

"French wine," Maddux said, shaking his head. "I can't believe this is Bearden's big idea, even less that it will work."

"Well, you don't know how much Jankovic loves

his French wine. In some reports I've read, several agents have suggested that he might be willing to trade prisoners for his favorite."

They neared the gates.

"You ready?" Dex asked. "Once we knock, there's no going back."

"Let's go get Pritchett."

Dex rapped on the gate, drawing the attention of a guard.

"State your name and business," he said in Serbian.

"I am Julien Durand here with my esteemed colleague Antoine Moreau," Dex said. "And we're here to speak with General Jankovic about some wine that we have available to him for a special price."

"Give me a minute," the guard said before scampering away to find Jankovic.

"Think he's buying this?" Maddux asked. "I still think the general might find it fishy that someone just comes and knocks on this gate trying to sell him some wine."

"I happen to think he's going to relish the opportunity to buy wine right here without having to travel into the city to get it."

"This whole mission is counting on you and Bearden being right about this," Maddux said.

"And it's also counting on you to deliver as a wine salesman. I make the introduction; you close the deal. That's how this works."

Maddux nodded. "Have you ever tried this stuff?"

"Once," Dex said. "I drank some at a party once while tailing a Russian ambassador who turned out to be a KGB agent."

"How was the wine?"

"It was good, although I wouldn't say it's worth the price you pay for it. But I'm a pretty simple guy who'd prefer a beer over anything else. You ever try it?"

Maddux shook his head. "I like wines, but I prefer a good glass of Scotch over any other drink, to be honest. However, I know enough about wines to be dangerous, maybe even get us in and out of trouble."

"I'll settle for the getting out of trouble part today."

They both stopped talking as the sound of rocks and dirt crunching under feet rapidly approached. The gate creaked as a guard swung it open. He pointed a rifle toward them, motioning for them to come inside.

Dex put his hands up and spoke in Serbian. "Can you please point your gun elsewhere? We are just wine salesmen making a special delivery for General Jankovic."

The guard obliged. "This way."

He led them through the prison, which Maddux observed to be more of a camp than a prison. There were high fences, but the prisoners were engaged in activities vital to the existence of the camp. Behind one building, a guard and two prisoners were hosing down pots and pans. Across from them, more prisoners carrying linens under the watch of a guard streamed into another structure. To Maddux's right, he heard the buzzing of a saw and the clanking of hammers. Maddux didn't remember reading about all the peripheral activities when perusing Bearden's report on his time at the Konjic prison.

Lugging the crate of wine, Maddux continued scanning the area for any other helpful intelligence regarding how the prison operated. He found the lack of yelling most odd, concluding that the facility was run more like a low-security detention facility than a tightly controlled prison. If the KGB was helping manage the prisoners, it wasn't with its well-documented iron fist.

A man who appeared to be in his early 50s approached Dex, Maddux, and their escort. Putting his hands on his hips, the newcomer furrowed his brow.

"General Jankovic," the guard said, nodding respectfully at the prison head. "This is Julien Durand and Antoine Moreau."

"So you are the two wine salesmen," Jankovic said in English.

"You speak English? We can speak Serbian if you prefer," Dex said.

"No," Jankovic said, shaking his head. "English is a far better language to use when discussing wine. And I hear you have some of my favorite, no?"

"Mouton Rothschild, vintage 1945," Dex said, grabbing a bottle from the crate and handing one to Jankovic.

Jankovic inspected the bottle for a moment to see if the label was authentic. "The victory year wine," he said with a sneer. "Are you trying to get me in trouble?"

"I'm sure once you taste this wine, you won't care when and where it came from—and neither would anyone else you offered it to."

Jankovic shrugged and continued to study the bottle of wine. "Very well then. Let's convene in my office."

They walked about a hundred meters back toward the entrance and then entered a building near the front. Jankovic led Dex and Maddux inside, offering them seats. Jankovic settled into the chair behind his desk and continued to look at the bottle.

"Before I buy, I try," Jankovic said. "That is my motto."

"Always sound advice," Maddux chimed in.

Jankovic reached into a desk drawer and produced a wine glass. He held it up to the light and proceeded to polish it. Satisfied that it was clean, he opened the top drawer and pulled out a bottle opener. He stood as he worked it into the cork before removing it with a loud pop. Wasting no time, he poured a generous portion and swirled it around before drinking.

When he was finished, Jankovic smacked his lips and let out a contented sigh. "Now, that is what I call a good glass of wine."

"Not an excellent glass of wine?" Dex asked.

"I don't like to use words like excellent," Jankovic said. "What if something better comes along? I choose to use my superlatives carefully."

Dex eyed Jankovic. "So you like it?"

"I love it," Jankovic said. "How much do you have?"

"How much do you want?"

"We have two dozen bottles, but—"

"I'll take them all," Jankovic said.

"Are you sure? This wine isn't cheap."

Jankovic chuckled. "I have money. I'll pay you what it cost. That's why you came here, no?"

Dex nodded. "This sounds like a deal. Unfortunately, I don't have all two dozen wine bottles here today. I only brought six and they come in individual crates."

"That should be enough for tonight," Jankovic said

with a laugh and a wink. "You can bring me the rest tomorrow."

Dex and Maddux followed Jankovic outside. Maddux felt satisfied that their reconnaissance mission inside the prison had been a success. He had a better idea for how the prison operated and what opportunities they had for sneaking Pritchett out. However, that was the lone item missing from their checklist: confirm Pritchett's presence.

As they walked across the yard, Maddux scanned the area and spotted Pritchett before he disappeared behind one of the buildings. He was wearing his hook, which was covered by what looked like a wine cork.

"General, we will need some help carrying the crates back inside," Maddux said. "Would it be possible to borrow some of your men to help us with them to speed the process along?"

Jankovic shrugged. "No problem." He turned toward one of the guards and gave him instructions.

Three prisoners hustled over to help tote the wine to Jankovic's office. Maddux handed over the crates, saving one for himself and Dex. Jankovic escorted the group.

Maddux nodded toward Pritchett. "Did you capture a pirate?"

Jankovic furrowed his brow. "I don't talk about the prisoners with outsiders. Understand?"

Maddux nodded. He had hoped to get Pritchett called over to them by Jankovic, maybe even have him make Pritchett do something. But that clearly wasn't going to happen. After placing the wine crate on Jankovic's desk with all the others, Maddux turned toward the door.

"We will return tomorrow with the rest," Dex said. "You can pay us then."

"I will have the money ready," Jankovic said. He ordered one of the guards to show Dex and Maddux to the gate.

Once outside, they climbed back into their car and headed to their hotel.

"That went well," Maddux said, glancing in the side mirror.

Dex shifted gears. "We got inside, if that's what you mean. But I didn't see Pritchett."

"You didn't? He was out in the main yard, visible for about ten seconds or so."

"What was he doing?"

"Looked like he was working with the linens."

"Is it me, or does that place not look like any prison you've ever seen? All the prisoners just seemed way too compliant, especially if they were apprehended by either the SDB or the KGB. They usually aren't criminals at all."

"So, what? They'd all be angry and give the guards a harder time?"

Dex nodded. "Exactly. But these guys were all just happy as could be, calmly carrying out their tasks as if it was something they enjoyed doing."

"Think they're experimenting on them? Maybe some mind-control techniques?"

"Maybe. I just know something isn't right."

Maddux glanced in his side mirror again. "That isn't the only thing that isn't right. Looks like we've got a tail."

Dex cursed as he downshifted. "What does this guy want?"

"Why don't you lose him? This car can run."

"That would defeat the purpose of everything we just did. We're trying to build Jankovic's trust so we can possibly get Pritchett out of there. If we run, he'll suspect us."

"And if we don't, he's liable to have us shot on sight, if anything just to get his hands on that wine."

"He won't do that because he'd hate to have his reputation tarnished among wine sellers across the region as someone who just might murder them. He's going to pay us."

"Unless we were made."

"Nobody made us, that much I'm sure of. Just let me handle these guys."

Dex drove calmly back to the hotel as they discussed their options for getting Pritchett out. After a few minutes, their car lurched to a stop in the hotel parking lot, and the guard who had been following them skidded to a stop in the spot to their left.

"Did you secure the weapons in the hiding spot?" Dex asked.

Maddux nodded. "But that doesn't mean he won't still find them."

"Well, if he does, we're done here—not to mention that he might kill us."

"I've got an idea. You do the talking, but follow my lead."

Dex shot Maddux a sideways glance. "I hope you know what you're doing."

The two agents stepped out of the car and looked in the direction of the guard. He opened his door and stood. Maddux estimated the man to be at least six-foot-three, maybe even taller.

"Can we help you?" Dex asked in Serbian.

"My boss sent me to check on you, to make sure you were real wine sellers," he said, struggling to speak in English.

"We're definitely real," Dex said. "Would you like to touch us?"

The guard cracked a faint smile. "Open up your trunk."

Dex walked around to the back and slid the key into the lock, turning it until the latch gave way and the trunk sprang open.

"Have a look for yourself," Dex said, gesturing toward the trunk.

Maddux slipped inside the main office and grabbed a cup of coffee. No cream, no sugar. Straight black, just like he took it. But this cup wasn't for him.

Maddux crowded up next to the guard, who was rifling through everything that had been stuffed inside.

"Not much in there but dirty clothes and fine wine, quite the combination," Maddux said.

The guard spun around, hitting his head on the trunk as he did. He let out a slight yelp in pain before turning to face Maddux. However, Maddux had encroached so close into the guard's space that he didn't see the cup of coffee. Maddux's drink spilled all over the man, resulting in louder yells.

"Hot, hot," the guard said, hopping around from one foot to the other.

"I'm so sorry," Maddux said. "Let me get you something to dry off with."

Maddux rushed inside and returned shortly with a towel he got from the man at the front desk.

"I hope this helps," Maddux said, blotting the guard's jacket. "I really hope you don't get in trouble for going back to the prison with a soiled jacket."

The guard waved Maddux off. "It's fine. Tomorrow the linen truck comes and cleans our uniforms. No one will notice."

"You don't do your own laundry?" Maddux asked. "I've never heard of such a thing."

"Only the guard's uniforms are cleaned outside the prison. It keeps the prisoners away from our uniforms."

"So they won't pull a prank?" Maddux asked.

The guard furrowed his brow, as if searching for the meaning of the word. "Prank?"

"A joke you do to someone to embarrass them or get back at them," Maddux said. "Ever heard of it?"

The guard shook his head. "No, but I know what you mean."

"Well, I apologize again for spilling coffee on your shirt," Maddux said. "I hope you have a good day."

The guard arched his eyebrows. "You think I am finished? I haven't checked underneath here yet." He tapped the bottom of the trunk.

Dex shot a glance at Maddux, who shrugged.

"Sometimes people try to deceive us. But they never deceive Boris."

"Boris?" Maddux asked.

The man tapped his chest. "*I* am Boris. And if you are hiding something, I will find it."

XXIII

PRITCHETT REACHED INTO THE BIN and pulled out a pile of sheets with his hook. With a snap of his wrist, he hurled the linens across the room toward another prisoner who shoved them into a washer. He stopped for a moment to mop his brow covered in sweat due to the steam swirling around the building.

"Keep working," one of the guards shouted at Pritchett.

He glanced at the guard, who glared back.

"Some of these guards are just wound too tight," a man whispered.

Pritchett turned to see an unexpected face—Harvey Cordell.

"Harvey—what are you doing here?" Pritchett asked softly.

"Don't stop what you're doing," Cordell said. "I wouldn't want you to get yelled at again."

The two men continued their duty of retrieving whatever items at the bottom of their baskets and tossing them over to the fellow prisoner responsible for loading each machine. As Pritchett surveyed the room, he noticed how listless the other prisoners were. And while the guards were attentive, they hardly looked in any other direction except Pritchett's.

"How did you end up here?" Cordell asked.

"No idea. I was in Barcelona for the race on a mission."

"I miss racing," Cordell said. "Kensington got me into it, but I haven't followed it closely in several months."

"Well, I'll break it down for you—a bunch of guys in fast cars go around and around. Eventually one of them crosses the finish line first."

"There's more to it than that. You're just—"

"I'm just not as impressed as most guys. It seems more like a hobby than a sport. And at the moment, you're going to have a hard time convincing me to enjoy it since one of the driver's is an assassin for the KGB, but I digress."

"So, what exactly happened to you?"

"The last thing I remember, I was being dragged away before waking up in the custody of some SDB agents."

"So, this wasn't the work of the KGB?"

Pritchett continued searching for laundry, speaking softly once his face was buried in the clothes bin. "I can't say for sure, but I'm sure they were working closely on this. My guess is that the KGB did this and I'm just being held here for a period of time."

"Well, someone is attempting to get you out," Cordell said.

"Really?"

"I saw two agents from the Bonn station here earlier—Poindexter and Maddux."

"Of course," Pritchett said. "Those two knuckle-heads are stupid enough and fiercely loyal to me that they would attempt such a thing. They're going to get caught."

"Maybe, maybe not. They seem to have a plan based around General Jankovic's weakness."

"Are they using wine?"

Cordell nodded. "That's a well-established fact within the agency. Looks like they sold him some."

"Did either Dex or Maddux see you?"

"No, I don't think so, but they're coming back very soon."

"How soon?"

"I overheard them say that they had some more bottles of wine to get for Jankovic. If they promised him some, I doubt they're going to want to keep him waiting."

"Yeah, we all know how he gets about his wine. If they don't get back here quickly, Jankovic will probably send someone after them."

"If they get captured, we'll likely never get out of here alive."

"That's the least of our worries," Pritchett said.

A guard stomped toward them, pointing as he spoke. "You and you—no talking."

Pritchett nodded and kept sorting. He waited until the guard was on the other side of the room at his post before resuming conversation again.

"That guy needs to be dealt with," Pritchett said, nodding in the guard's direction.

"Wait, back up a second," Cordell said. "What do you mean this is the least of our worries? For the time being, escaping is the biggest concern I have."

"Well, it shouldn't be. There's far more to this place than meets the eye."

Cordell pulled another cart over to them and continued sorting. "Please, enlighten me."

"Don't you see what's going on around you?"

Cordell scanned the room. "Looks like prison work detail to me."

Pritchett shook his head. "I've only got one eye and I can see what's happening better than you. Take another look."

Cordell went along. "Nope. I'm not seeing anything else."

"Everyone here is like a robot. They do exactly what they are told without questioning, without fighting. It's inane. This is not what defiance looks like."

"Maybe they're tired of resisting. Have you ever considered that?"

Pritchett sighed. "There's putting your head down and doing your work. And then there are vacant stares. Just look around, and you'll start to notice what I'm talking about."

Cordell shrugged. "I'm not seeing it."

"Hey, you," a guard barked as he pointed at Cordell. "I said no talking."

Cordell turned around and pointed at himself, feigning ignorance. "Me," he mouthed to the guard.

But he had already darted from his position and was hustling toward Cordell. With a forearm shiver to his face, Cordell tumbled to the ground. The guard kicked Cordell in the ribs.

"Next time, you obey," the guard said as he placed his foot on Cordell's chest.

Cordell nodded and coughed, clutching his midsection and glaring up at the guard.

"Get back to work," the guard said with a growl.

Cordell clambered to his feet, staggering for a few steps before grabbing on to one of the linen carts to help regain his balance.

Pritchett put his arm around Cordell to help him stand upright.

"See what I'm talking about?" Pritchett said. "They're treating us more harshly than anyone else here."

Cordell moaned softly. "Maybe you're right. I know my ribs will agree with anything you say right now."

Pritchett finished removing the last piece from the cart and wheeled them toward the back entrance, which contained a ramp for transporting objects up and down. He heard a pair of guards talking in Serbian, which made him freeze before busting through the door.

"How have the prisoners been?" one guard asked.

"They are a little ornery, but I've seen worse," the other replied.

"Like the Polish assassin?"

"We've never had anyone worse than him. Minding these two is a dream in comparison."

"Well, they won't be so feisty after tomorrow, will they?"

Pritchett put his shoulder into the swinging doors, whistling as he went. The guards scrambled to get out of the way, each muttering curses underneath his breath. With a forceful shove, Pritchett pushed the cart down the ramp where another prisoner stood mindlessly waiting.

Hustling back toward the main room, Pritchett signaled for Cordell to come over.

"What is it?" Cordell asked. "I'm really taking a big risk right now. This better be worth it."

"Something is going to happen to us by tomorrow," Pritchett said.

"And what exactly is going to happen?" Cordell asked.

"I don't know yet, but it's supposedly something to do with our behavior, which would make me right about what I said earlier. Whatever it is, it's going to make us more compliant like all these other prisoners."

"What are they going to do? Hypnotize us?" Cordell asked with a chuckle.

Pritchett glowered at him. "Don't mock. We have no idea what's truly going on in this facility—and I don't want to find out either, and I'm betting neither do you."

"Hey," the guard barked from across the room. "Didn't I say no talking?"

Pritchett looked around and pointed at himself. "Are you speaking to me?"

"You were talking, weren't you?"

Pritchett shrugged. "Depends on what you mean by the word *talking*."

"Shut up," the guard said. "Solitary confinement for you."

"No, no, no," Pritchett argued. "Neither one of us were talking."

"Let's go," said the guard, unwilling to listen to any of Pritchett's protests while shoving the Bonn station chief down a narrow corridor. "You'll be lucky to see sunshine in the next couple of weeks."

XXIV

MADDUX BUTTONED THE TOP button on his shirt and pulled it taut. He stared at the unfamiliar insignia on his sleeves then tugged on the cuffs. Wearing the enemy's uniform felt foreign to him, almost as if he were betraying his country. It felt almost as strange as the disguise he was sporting. Maddux smoothed his fake mustache as he went over a few more phrases in Serbian.

"You're getting the hang of the language," Dex said. "Don't be afraid to talk tonight. Be confident. If you mess something up, I'll cover for you."

Maddux nodded and looked back down at his shirt.

"Something about this doesn't seem right," Maddux said to Dex, who had also donned a uniform.

"First time going this undercover?" Dex asked.

"First time I've had to wear a uniform, if that's what you mean."

"It's all about confidence. If you look the part and act the part, no one is going to question you, especially at night. We just file in with all the rest of the guards during the shift change, and we'll be fine."

"And if something goes wrong?"

"We run like hell and pray neither of us gets shot in the back."

Maddux arched his eyebrows and cocked his head to one side. "That doesn't exactly instill a lot of confidence, now does it?"

"You got any better ideas at the moment?"

Maddux shook his head. "I just want to grab Pritchett and get out of here. Something's not right about this prison camp."

"Everyone does seem very compliant, don't they?"

"It's like the prisoners aren't even really there."

"Being in an environment like this will do that to you."

Maddux wagged his finger. "No, there's something different about this place. And I'm not sure what it is, but I don't like it."

"Well, hopefully we'll never have to come back after tonight."

* * *

AT THE GATE, Maddux and Dex joined in with the security detail entering the prison for the late night shift. Maddux gave his hat one final tug down low across his brow before falling in line. The guard on duty hardly seemed interested in checking anyone's credentials until Maddux and Dex prepared to pass by.

"Wait," the guard said in Serbian. "Identification?"

They held up their badges. Maddux swallowed hard, hoping nothing raised suspicion. The guard inspected it closely before releasing it and waving them inside.

Once they were in, a guard in front of them turned around.

"I don't believe I've seen you here before. Who are you?"

"We're here on assignment from Belgrade, just a routine checkup from headquarters," Dex said. "You should have nothing to worry about if you're doing your job."

The guard nodded. "Let me know if you need any assistance. I'll be happy to show you around."

"Why don't you show us the cells first?" Dex said. "We want to see how you're housing these criminals."

The guard grinned and offered his hand. "Happy to help. I am Braco Milovic. And you're in luck because I'm working in that building tonight. Just follow me."

He led them toward a nearby structure. When the guard at the door asked for their credentials, Milovic waved the man off. "They're from Belgrade on a routine inspection. I'm sure you don't want to trouble them."

The guard eyed Dex and Maddux.

"No need to worry," Dex said. "You followed protocol, but we would rather spend our time inspecting the facility rather than evaluating you."

The guard nodded and pushed a button, resulting in a loud buzz as the door unlocked.

Maddux estimated half of the men were asleep on their cots, while the other half sat still.

"As you can see, most of the men are well adjusted," Milovic said. "The program seems to be working."

"Indeed it does," Dex said.

"Do you have any new prisoners?" Maddux asked.

"You mean ones that haven't been programed yet?" Milovic responded.

"Of course," Maddux said.

"Right this way," Milovic said before turning down another corridor. "We have been waiting the prescribed number of days mandated by the KGB and taking note of any changes. But three days of rebellious behavior can seem like a long time when we're used to prisoners who are much more obedient."

"When are these soldiers scheduled to be programmed?" Dex asked.

"They will receive their first shots tonight, and then we'll complete the process tomorrow afternoon. I'm sure you know Dr. Stravinsky will be here to administer everything."

"Of course," Dex said. "Part of the reason we wanted to inspect tonight was to see how these prisoners acted before you began the programming."

"Well, they may be asleep," Milovic said. "There's no guarantees. But knowing how much trouble we had with one of these men last night, I would guess that he'll be all for making trouble now."

"What was he doing?" Maddux asked.

"I don't know, but I know he angered General Jankovic," Milovic said. "We were instructed to keep an eye on him, which is quite funny, if you ask me."

"Funny? How?" Maddux asked.

"Well, this prisoner only has one eye," Milovic said as a grin spread across his face. "So, it is only necessary to keep one eye on him."

"Never underestimate what a non-programmed prisoner can do," Dex said.

Milovic stopped in front of an empty cell. "Well, that's strange. He's not here."

"Did they transfer him?" Maddux asked.

"He wasn't scheduled to be transferred. Perhaps he's getting his shots."

A flashlight down the hall arrested their attention.

"Milovic," called a fellow guard. "If you're looking for this prisoner, he's been moved to solitary confinement."

"What did he do?" Milovic asked.

"General disobedience. Talking when he wasn't supposed to be."

"And the other new guy?"

"He's in the other wing. Want me to take these men to him? I heard they're visiting from Belgrade."

"Yes, they are, but I can handle it," Milovic said. "Thank you for the update."

"Any time," the guard said as he turned and walked away.

"This way," Milovic said, motioning for Dex and Maddux to follow. "It's a little bit of a walk to the other wing, but we'll go there first before going to solitary."

Maddux shot a knowing look at Dex. Neither of them were interested in the other new prisoner. All they wanted was Pritchett.

By the time they arrived in the other wing, Maddux was itching to leave. Their window for snatching Pritchett was shrinking. It was only a matter of time before someone higher up in the chain of authority learned about the presence of the two inspectors from Belgrade and questioned them more thoroughly.

The prisoner lunged at them when Milovic shined a light in his eyes.

"See," Milovic said. "He'll act very differently tomorrow night. We only have to endure this behavior a little while longer."

Neither Maddux nor Dex recognized the man.

"And the other prisoner?" Maddux asked.

"Let me take you to him."

A three-minute walk through down various hallways led them to solitary confinement. Maddux thought how eerie it was to be in a place so quiet all alone yet surrounded by armed guards on the other side of the walls.

Milovic flashed his light as they entered the hallway leading to the cell. "This particular area is lit only by natural light. We find that the darkness keeps the prisoners calmer."

He lit up a man sitting on his cot.

"See," Milovic said. "Very calm, though he wasn't earlier today, which is obviously why he's here."

"Can we speak with him?" Dex asked. "We have a few questions."

"Be my guest," Milovic said.

"No, inside. I want to go inside and speak with him."

Maddux watched Pritchett, who used his forearm to shield against the light. Maddux figured Pritchett still couldn't tell who they were.

"I don't think that's a good idea," Milovic said.

"He's got one arm and one eye," Dex said. "How difficult could he be to handle?"

Milovic sighed and pulled out his keys. "Fine. But if something happens to him, it's on you. Here. Hold my flashlight on the lock."

Dex nodded at Maddux, who took up a position to Milovic's right. Dex waited until he heard the lock click before springing into action.

Maddux grabbed the door, bracing it for impact. A half second later, Milovic's head bounced against it, complements of Dex. Knocked out cold, Milovic crumpled to the floor.

"We've got to move," Dex said to Pritchett.

"I hope you have a plan to get Cordell out of here too."

"Harvey Cordell? He's in here?" Dex asked.

Pritchett nodded as he watched Dex and Maddux strip the guard. "I ran into him yesterday."

"Just start getting undressed," Dex said. "We can talk about this later."

Pritchett started unbuttoning his shirt but was resistant to the idea of tabling the conversation. "We can't just leave Cordell. They're doing some crazy stuff in here."

"We know," Dex said. "They're programming people."

"I knew," Pritchett said, snapping his fingers. "This place is experimenting on prisoners."

"You were going to begin the process tonight," Maddux began, "which is why we need to hustle and get out of here."

"So, we're just going to walk out the front gate and leave him behind?" Pritchett asked as he pulled on the guard's pants.

"We never planned on rescuing Cordell. That would put everything else in jeopardy if we did," Dex said.

"Besides, it would be too risky to take Cordell since he's already been programmed," Maddux added.

"What are you talking about? Cordell is fine. They haven't done anything to him yet."

"Are you sure about that?" Dex asked.

"Yeah, I spoke with him earlier today," Pritchett said. "In fact, it's why I'm in solitary. I was talking to him after I was warned to stop talking."

Maddux handed Pritchett the guard's jacket. "That's not our understanding. The little tour we just took thanks to our napping guard here said that there were only two prisoners who hadn't been programmed. We met the other one, and he wasn't Cordell."

"Then Cordell must be the mole," Dex said. "That's the only thing that makes sense."

"No, I've known Cordell forever. He wouldn't do something like that," Pritchett said.

Dex shook his head. "You've been in this business far longer than I have, yet you couldn't concede that Cordell might be the man who's been sharing all our secrets with the KGB? You never *really* know about people, especially your fellow spies."

"I trained Cordell myself. I don't care what you say; I know it's not him," Pritchett said as he finished getting dressed. "And I'm not leaving without him."

"You are tonight if you want to leave with us," Dex said. "This is not up for debate."

Pritchett grunted. "You're making a big mistake."

"If you can prove that Cordell isn't the mole, we'll come back tomorrow. Otherwise, we're out of here," Dex said.

"Well, how the hell am I going to do that right now?" Pritchett asked.

"I've got an idea," Maddux said to Pritchett. "But first, you might want to throw your jacket over your arm and remove your patch. We're going to look suspicious enough as it is."

Pritchett took Maddux's suggestion. "I may only have one hand, but with my hook, I'm fully armed."

"Stay close," Dex said. "I hope we don't need it, but you never know."

Dex snatched the rest of Milovic's keys off his belt and chained him to the cot. They locked the cell door and then secured the door to the solitary confinement cell. No one would know Milovic was missing until someone delivered a meal in the morning.

They hustled down the hallway and exited through the other wing. The guard posted near the door was reading a magazine and barely glanced up to see them. Once they reached the courtyard, Maddux explained his plan and headed toward the main office.

"Hold up just a minute," Maddux said. "I need to do something."

He hustled over to a nearby transport vehicle and slipped the bomb Rose had given him beneath the carriage.

"What was that for?" Dex asked. "We don't really want to make a scene."

"Not unless we have to," Maddux said. "Now let's keep moving."

Once they reached the office, Maddux volunteered to go inside.

"Why don't you two take a smoke break while I handle this one on my own?" he asked.

Dex and Pritchett didn't protest, settling onto a bench adjacent to the door, while Maddux went inside.

Behind a counter stood a guard who sported wisps of gray hair protruding from beneath his cap.

"Can I help you?" he asked. "Wait, who are you? Are you one of the new trainees?"

Maddux shook his head. "I'm from the main office in Belgrade. Just here doing a routine inspection tonight."

"Nobody told me anything about that."

Maddux leaned onto the counter and leaked a wry smile before speaking in a whisper. "That's because if someone told you we were coming, you wouldn't be carrying on as usual. You'd be on your best behavior, putting your best foot forward, all in an effort to impress me. This way I just know how you operate under normal circumstances."

The guard nodded. "I see. Well, in that case, what can I do for you?"

"I need to see the file of a prisoner named Harvey Cordell."

"Let me see what I can find," the guard said before turning around and rifling through the filing cabinet behind him.

Maddux drummed his fingers on the counter while he waited. Half a minute later, the guard spun around and slid a folder to Maddux.

"That's all we've got on him right there," the guard said.

Maddux opened up the file and froze, stymied by the daunting task of reading everything written in Serbian. Speaking the language was one thing, but reading it presented a different challenge, a far more difficult challenge.

"How long has Cordell been here?" Maddux asked.

The guard stood and leaned over the counter,

pointing toward the date box. "He came in a couple weeks ago."

Maddux started doing the math in his head. If Cordell had been there two weeks before, it would co-incide with the time of his disappearance. Yet if Cordell was a double agent, what was he doing in an SDB prison?

"Do you know why he was brought in?" Maddux asked.

The guard sighed. "You really need to learn how to read one of these reports." He stood again and pointed to another box. "Right there. It says a man named Kensington brought him in."

Maddux tried not to let his surprise show.

XXV

JOVAN"COME ON," MADDUX SAID. "We need to get moving."

He grabbed Pritchett's arm and ushered him to his feet. Dex rose slowly, but Maddux was already motioning for his colleague to hurry.

"We've got to get out of here," Maddux said in a whisper.

"What did you find?" Dex asked. "Was I right?"

"Pritchett was right. Cordell isn't a traitor, but we'll put everything at risk if we go back now. We can get him tomorrow."

"How do you intend to do that?" Pritchett asked.

"Just leave the details to us," Dex said. "I'm sure our little genius here has a plan."

"Mock me all you want, Dex, but I found out more than just the truth about whether or not Cordell was a traitor. I learned the identity of the mole."

Pritchett stopped. "Who is it?"

Maddux tugged on Pritchett again. "Keep walking, and act normal."

"Who is it?" Pritchett demanded.

"Kensington," Maddux said as he kept his eyes affixed on the gate less than a hundred meters away.

"Walt Kensington? The station chief in Belgrade?" Dex asked.

"The one and only," Maddux said. "Just keep walking, and I'll fill you in on all the details later."

A few seconds later, Maddux heard the shouts of another man from behind them in the courtyard.

"Don't turn around," Maddux said.

"What did you do?" Pritchett asked.

"Nothing, but we don't have time to stop. They're going to figure out who we are if stick around here much longer. Just keep moving."

The guard behind them insisted, compelling Maddux to stop and turn around. His eyes widened as he noticed a man with his arm raised, hustling toward them. But it was the scene behind him that made Maddux's throat tighten—General Jankovic strode determinedly toward them.

"We probably should run," Dex said.

Maddux gestured for everyone to stay where they were and remain calm. "I'll handle this. Don't blow our cover just yet."

"General Jankovic wants to speak with you," the aide said. "Please wait."

Jankovic and his man were some fifty meters away but closing fast. Maddux stuck his hand into his pocket and grabbed the small device. He flicked open the protective covering and pressed the button.

A loud explosion rocked the courtyard as the transport vehicle flew several meters into the air before crashing back down to the ground. Flames consumed the truck, and another explosion followed.

"Don't go anywhere," Jankovic yelled.

"Go, now," Maddux said. The three men resumed their exit, walking swiftly toward the car. Once they got inside, they raced down the road and headed straight for the motel.

"All right, Maddux, tell us what you found out."

Maddux related his interaction with the office guard and what was in the files.

"I swear, Kensington ought to swing for this," Pritchett said.

"Well, that's not the least of our concerns," Maddux said, looking at Pritchett. "We've got Cordell stuck in there. And while they likely won't figure out that you're gone until the morning, as soon as Jankovic figures out what happened, that place is going to be crawling with SDB agents. We're going to need to get back in there first thing to get Cordell out. Got any ideas?"

Pritchett furrowed his brow. "I thought you had a big idea."

"Well, I do, sort of," Maddux stammered. "It's just that—it's just that I needed to keep you moving or else they would've been all over us."

Pritchett sighed. "Well, the only thing I can think of is that the linens truck for all the guards was scheduled to show up tomorrow morning at eight o'clock."

"That'll work," Dex said. "We just need to figure out a way to get a message to Cordell and create a diversion to get him into the truck."

"I think I know exactly how we can do this," Maddux said.

* * *

A FEW MINUTES BEFORE 8:00 A.M., Maddux and Dex returned to the prison as the wine-selling tandem of Durand and Moreau. Dex rapped on the gate, startling a sleepy-eyed guard.

"What is this all about?" the guard asked. "We're not expecting any deliveries until 8:00 a.m."

"We're early," Dex said.

"And who are you?"

"I am Julien Durand, and this is my colleague Antoine Moreau. We're here to meet with General Jankovic."

The guard glanced at his clipboard. "Two things. First of all, I don't see you on the list. Secondly, no one disturbs General Jankovic until he's eaten breakfast. That's a hard-fast rule."

"This is about wine," Dex countered. "I suggest you go and get him because he'll want to receive this shipment."

"I could receive it for him," the guard offered.

"No, it must be signed and received by the general," Dex said. "Besides, he needs to settle his bill."

"If he hasn't emerged from his quarters, he hasn't finished breakfast," the guard said. "There isn't anything I can do."

Dex dug into his pocket and grabbed a fistful of cash. He slapped it into the guard's hand.

"Still nothing you can do about it?" Dex asked.

The guard smiled. "I'll be right back."

A couple minutes later, Dex saw the guard walking toward the entrance with Jankovic, whose eyes were narrowed beneath a furrowed brow.

"I wonder what he's so happy about?" Maddux asked.

"Brace yourself," Dex said. "This isn't going to be pretty."

The guard flung open the gate but kept his gun trained on the two visitors.

"We need to make this snappy," Jankovic said. "We had an incident last night here at the prison, and I have much to do."

Before Dex could respond, the linen truck rolled up behind them.

Maddux glanced at his watch and smiled. *Right on schedule.*

They all shuffled to the side to allow the truck to enter.

"We have quite a few bottles for you, so we just need to know where to put them," Dex said. "Once we do that, we can settle up our accounts and get out of your way."

"We'll put the wine in my office," Jankovic said. "I cleared out a spot for it until I can move it all to my personal cellar."

Dex nodded, and he and Maddux started the unloading process. One by one, they carried the wine up a gently sloping hill to Jankovic's office. As they walked, Maddux scanned the commons area for Cordell. By the third trip, Maddux noticed him and said something to Jankovic, who had remained in his office doing paperwork.

"Do you think there's any chance we could get some help?" Maddux asked. "We would love to get out of your way sooner,"

"What do you need?" Jankovic asked.

"Maybe a couple men to help lug these crates up here."

"Fine," Jankovic said before instructing the guard posted at his door to accommodate Maddux's request.

Once they stepped back outside, Maddux pointed in Cordell's direction. "What about those two men over there?"

The guard shrugged before calling over Cordell and another man. After receiving instructions on what to do, the two prisoners hustled over to Maddux and Dex.

"That was easy enough," Dex said. "But don't be fooled. Things are never easy."

"Tell me about it," Maddux said as he handed a crate to Cordell.

It took less than ten minutes to finish the job lugging all the wine crates up to Jankovic's office. All that remained was to collect the payment.

Dex knocked on Jankovic's office. "General, we wanted to let you know that we've delivered all the bottles as promised and would like to get back on the road. We have more places to visit in the coming days."

Jankovic smiled. "I don't want to hold you." He stood and opened up a safe in the wall, carefully guarding against them seeing the combination..

Dex gave him a total. The amount was the same as what they paid for the wine. Jankovic sifted through stacks of cash until he reached the agreed upon amount.

"Thank you, sir," Dex said as he received the money. "I hope you have a better day than you did last night."

"What are you talking about?" Jankovic asked, feigning ignorance.

"The guard up front mentioned you had an

incident here," Dex said, covering quickly for his misstep.

"No, everything here was quiet last night," Jankovic said. "He must have been mistaken. Which guard told you this again?"

"The one at the main gate," Dex said. "But don't get him in trouble. I shouldn't have said anything."

Jankovic laughed softly. "There's nothing to worry about because nothing happened. But thank you for thinking of me, and I look forward to seeing you again in the future when you return."

Dex pocketed the money and headed out the door with Maddux.

Maddux stole a quick glance over his shoulder in the direction of the linens truck. The driver climbed behind the wheel, and the truck roared to life. As Maddux walked toward the gate, the truck veered past them, its brakes squeaking as a guard stood at the exit holding up both hands.

"Is there a problem?" the driver asked.

"No problem," the guard said. "Just the same procedure we follow every time you leave. We need to check your truck."

Three guards swarmed on the truck, yanking open the back doors and sifting through all the laundry. Once they were satisfied, they moved on to the sides of the truck. They used poles with angled mirrors attached to the end to see underneath.

Maddux paused to watch the inspection unfold, but the entire scene became chaotic when Jankovic stormed out of his office, ranting about something.

"We need to move," Dex said. "Now."

They hustled toward their car. Dex wasted no time

in firing up the engine before stomping on the gas. Dirt and gravel sprayed the prison fence as the car lurched forward and snaked onto the road. Maddux looked back over his shoulder just in time to see Jankovic pointing a gun at someone before pulling the trigger.

"That bastard just shot someone, didn't he?" Dex asked.

Maddux was slow to respond, drinking in the escalating scene behind them.

"Probably the guard I ratted out," Dex said.

"I didn't think Jankovic would—" Maddux let his words hang, realizing that he actually wasn't surprised.

"You're smarter than that," Dex said. "I knew he would kill the guy. Casualty of the game."

Maddux bit his lip, disappointed in both Jankovic's malicious handling of the situation and Dex's callous dismissal of a man he practically sentenced to death.

"Don't lose too much sleep over it," Dex said. "This is what happens in our world."

After five minutes of bumping along the private road leading to the prison, Dex skidded to a stop. He got out, unlatched the hood, and propped it up.

"You think the linen truck will stop?" Maddux asked.

"I'll do my best to make sure he does," Dex said, opening the trunk and pulling out a set of tools.

Another five minutes passed, then ten. Still no truck.

"You think something happened?" Maddux asked. "Maybe they found Cordell."

"Cordell knows what he's doing. If he didn't want to be found, he avoided all their detection devices."

"I hope you're right."

The seconds dripped past as Maddux imagined the worst. Dex leaned against the side of the car, relaxed and ready for the next portion of their operation.

"How do you handle all of this?" Maddux asked, breaking the silence.

"Handle all of what?" Dex asked.

"You know, the death, the anxiety, the uncertainty—because I don't want to become numb to it all."

Dex nodded knowingly. "You have to stay numb when things go wrong in order to stay alive. And we're staying alive because we want our loved ones to stay alive—that's how you do it. Think about everything you do as a sacrifice for them, the people back home who have no idea this shadow world exists. While they're all worried about job security and inflation and how they're going to afford their next car, we're out here keeping them safe. And if you don't think that way, you'll either fall prey to the lure of money or disappear into the pit of despair."

"You've really thought this through, haven't you?"

"You can't do the things I've done without spending a substantial amount of time thinking about why you're doing what you're doing. You know, like the time you spend tied up in a wine cellar because a fellow agent thinks you're out to kill him."

Maddux shot Dex a sideways glance. Dex flashed a smile.

"Don't worry," Dex said, "I'm over it. But I will get you back one day when you aren't looking."

Maddux wasn't sure if Dex was joking or not. The wry smile on his face left his true frame of mind ambiguous.

Before Maddux could respond, the sound of an approaching truck just beyond the hill behind them arrested both agents' attention.

"Looks like we have company," Dex said. "Get ready."

Maddux walked around their car, kicking the tires. Dex tightened his rolled up sleeves and hung his head. He looked up as the linens truck drew nearer, raising his hand to flag it down. The truck slowed to a halt, the engine still running.

"Is there a problem?" the driver asked.

"I think it's the carburetor, but I don't have the proper wrench to loosen it. Do you happen to have a tool set in your truck?"

The man, whose eyes were distant and face pale, nodded. "I think I have something I can give you to help."

"That was crazy back there, wasn't it?" Dex said.

The driver nodded. "I've witnessed three guards getting killed over the past six months—and it bothers me just the same every time."

"It's a wild world we live in, isn't it?" Maddux asked.

"I hope this place is better off when my daughter gets older," the driver said.

"Oh, you have a little girl?" Maddux asked.

The man nodded as he dug through his toolbox. "She's only nine months old and so innocent. I would hate for her to see all the things I've seen in this country."

"Maybe things will get better," Dex said.

The man handed over a wrench set. "Is this what you're looking for?"

Dex nodded. "Perfect. Just give me a second."

The driver sat on the tailgate, hindering Maddux's plan. Cordell was supposed to crawl out, but he needed to do it without the driver in view. Yet with him still outside the truck, the opportunity wasn't there.

"See if that works," Dex said.

Maddux hustled over to the car, sliding behind the steering wheel. He turned the engine, and their car roared to life.

Dex let out a celebratory yelp before working quickly to reattach the cover to the carburetor. He slid the socket back into its case and handed it over to the driver.

"I appreciate your help," Dex said.

The man took the tools and put them away. "Safe travels, gentlemen." He climbed back behind the steering wheel and eased onto the gas. The truck gained speed, rambling along the dirt road.

Maddux and Dex scanned the area.

"Where the hell is Cordell?" Dex asked.

Maddux's eyes widened as he searched for their colleague, but he wasn't in plain view.

XXVI

MADDUX SIGHED as he climbed into the passenger's side. Dex slammed the dashboard with both fists and let fly a few choice words. He launched into a rant about how they risked their lives for Cordell, and he ignored them.

"Maybe he's the real mole," Dex said aloud as if he were having an epiphany.

"Then why wouldn't he have ratted us out?" Maddux asked. "It would've been easy for him to do it."

Dex jammed his foot on the gas, sending rocks and dirt flying.

"Calm down," Maddux said. "You don't know what happened. Let's not jump to any conclusions just yet."

As they came around the bend, a thump hit the side of their car. Dex slammed on the brakes and brought the vehicle to a halt.

"That son of a—" Dex said, winding up for another rant. He stopped when he saw Cordell stand along the side of the road.

"I told you not to jump to any conclusions," Maddux said with a wink.

Cordell flung the door open and eased inside. "Is anyone behind us?"

Dex looked in the rearview mirror. "Looks clear to me."

"I'm still staying down," Cordell said. "Who knows how many men Jankovic will have out looking for me once they realize I'm gone."

"Well, we're going to swing back by the hotel and pick up Pritchett before we stuff you two away in that cozy spot in the back," Maddux said.

"That's all I need after holding on for dear life to that truck axel," Cordell said.

"You did good," Dex said. "Once we cross the border, you'll have to fill us in on everything that happened."

* * *

THE MEETING THE NEXT afternoon in Bonn was tense. Everyone was happy to see Pritchett back in his office and Cordell extracted from the SDB prison. But an angst still hung in the air, knowing that Medved and possibly other Russian super assassins were still out there, not to mention the fact that one of their own was working for the KGB.

"We still haven't found Medved," Bearden began. "All our agents are still in danger as long as he's out there."

"There is no Medved," Cordell said as he leaned forward in his chair.

Every person in the room turned and looked at Cordell, waiting for someone to ask the lingering question everyone wanted to know the answer to.

"But what about your report? There's still a Russian super assassin running around, no?" Bearden asked.

Cordell shook his head. "It's all just fantasy."

"But I read your report and—"

"No, you read Kensington's report. He's been behind this the entire time. But he made one big mistake."

"What's that?" Bearden asked.

"He let me live."

Maddux scratched down a few notes on the paper in front of him. He heard the entire story on the road trip back from Yugoslavia. It seemed just as unfathomable now.

"So, let me get this straight," Bearden said. "Kensington apprehended you and turned you over to the KGB?"

Cordell nodded.

"Then they took you to an SDB detention camp where they were conducting experiments but didn't experiment on you?"

"Yes," Cordell said, rotating his coffee cup slightly with his left hand. "Apparently, I was supposed to be programmed like everyone else, and somehow it just slipped through the cracks. One of the guards informed me on the morning of my escape that I was needed at noon for a special examination. I'd heard that term bandied around enough to know what they were planning on doing. I guess someone noted it in my file from the night before and it was brought to the attention of a supervising officer."

Bearden held his thumb and index finger barely apart. "So you were *this* close to getting your mind melted?"

"If Dex and Maddux here hadn't pulled this off, I would be robotic by now."

"Looks like you have a lot to be thankful for," Bearden said. "Now, let's get down to brass tacks, shall we? How do we catch Kensington?"

* * *

AROUND NOON the next day, Maddux sauntered to the CIA offices and slipped into a chair in Pritchett's office. He was buried in a stack of paperwork and barely looked up to acknowledge his civilian agent.

"I want in on tracking down Kensington," Maddux said.

"Of course you do," Pritchett said. "But I'm going to let Dex handle this one on his own. We don't need a big footprint."

"I understand, sir. But I need to talk to Kensington first."

Pritchett looked up and adjusted his eye patch. "What for? To ask him about your father?"

"Is that surprising to you?"

"Of course not. I would expect nothing less from you." He paused and looked back down at his documents. "The answer is still no."

"Oh, come on, sir. You know the links between my father and others in the CIA are scarce. If Kensington can help me connect some dots, then maybe—"

"Just stop yourself right there," Pritchett said. "Ask yourself *why* Kensington would help you when he just betrayed his country. Then ask yourself how you could believe a single word out of his mouth as he was playing us for fools. I think after you honestly answer those questions, you'll see why I think it's foolish for you to go anywhere right now."

"He'll talk to me," Maddux said. "I know he will."

"No, you hope he'll talk to you. You think that you can persuade him to give you the information you want, but you would be mistaken."

"Just give me a chance."

"The answer is final," Pritchett said as he reached for his stamp and slammed it down on top of the paper he was reading. "Now take some time off. I don't want to see you around here until next week at the earliest, understand?"

Maddux sighed then nodded before standing up and leaving. He was more determined than ever to venture back into Belgrade and find Kensington. Maddux wasn't sure he'd get what he was looking for when he got there, but that wasn't the only reason he felt compelled to ignore Pritchett's orders.

XXVII

MADDUX PERUSED THE WINE list as he waited on Rose to join him at his second-favorite restaurant, Sudhaus. He enjoyed the veal schnitzel so much that he didn't mind the half-hour cab ride to get there. After visiting the establishment for the third time, he claimed the booth in the back corner as his territory. The wait staff caught on to his preferred seating arrangement and made sure he sat there whenever possible. And it was open when he arrived.

He ordered a bottle of wine, one he knew Rose would enjoy, and scanned the menu. However, his interest in the food selection was feigned. There was only one thing he ever ate—veal schnitzel. He talked so much about how delicious it was that he'd convinced Pritchett to try it as well, though the station chief didn't find the entree as delectable as Maddux did.

After another five minutes, Rose finally arrived. Maddux stood and greeted her with a cordial hug before gesturing for her to sit down.

"I already ordered us a bottle of wine," he said.

"Nice," she said, rubbing her hands together. "So, what are we celebrating?"

"Nothing in particular, maybe the fact that I'm still alive."

"That's always a good thing," she said as she placed her napkin in her lap. "Why don't we also celebrate the fact that we are both employed as well after tying up a fellow agent and leaving him in a wine cellar."

Maddux chuckled. "And that he forgave us."

"Dex is a good agent," Rose said. "I'm not sure I would've responded like he did."

The waiter approached their table, carrying the wine. He poured a healthy portion in both of their glasses and quickly left.

"On that note, I propose a toast to our colleague, who isn't with us tonight," Maddux said as he raised his glass. "To Dex."

They clinked their glasses before taking a swig of the merlot.

"So, why did you want to meet with me for dinner tonight?" Rose asked.

"I need you to do me a favor."

"Of course. You know I'm happy to help you any time I can."

"It's a little bit tricky, so don't agree just yet."

"I'm sure I can handle it. What do you need?"

Maddux exhaled slowly after a deep breath. "Pritchett told me to take some time off and not go in the office for a week. I don't know if he's afraid I'm getting burned out or if he thinks I made too many mistakes on this last mission."

"But you can't do that, can you?"

"No, I can't. And it has to do with Dex walking into a trap."

"A trap? What are you talking about?"

"Call it a hunch, but there's something not right about how this whole situation unfolded."

Rose smiled. "The last time you had a hunch, we tied up Dex."

Maddux narrowed his eyes and shook his head. "This is different."

"I'm not trying to be belligerent when I ask this, but are you sure?"

"No, which is why I need your help. I need you to confirm my suspicions."

"And what do you suspect at the moment?"

"I don't want to tell you until I see the documents that I need you to get. I don't want to mess this up. The consequences are too severe."

"So what papers do you need?"

"I want to see the original message passed from the Belgrade station to Pritchett in Venice. And not the transcribed, typewritten one either. I need the original handwritten note."

"Anything else I can get for you?" she asked with a chuckle. "A car, a plane, a rocket launcher."

"Well, since you asked, there is one device I'd like you to get for me. You know that sonic transmitter that cripples just about everyone in range?"

"Oh, how could I forget?"

"I'd like to get that as well fitted inside a pair of dress shoes. I wear a size 12."

"I'll see what I can do," she said. "But I'm not sure it will be all that easy."

"I need everything by tomorrow morning."

Rose's eyes widened. "Tomorrow morning? Are you planning on going somewhere?"

"If what's on that document is what I think, I'll be headed to Belgrade."

"What on earth for?"

"To kill Medved."

* * *

THE NEXT MORNING, Maddux walked by the CIA offices and conducted a brush pass with Rose. She casually dropped a shoebox into Maddux's shopping bag as she walked by, refusing to make eye contact with him. Maddux hustled back to his office at Opel and opened the package.

He sat down in his chair to read the papers but first came across a note Rose left attached with a paperclip in the upper left hand corner.

"I need these back in one hour. Same protocol for returning as for receiving."

She didn't write her name or even use her initial, but it didn't matter. Rose's distinct handwriting was regularly lauded at the agency. When all the other agents and staff members looked like they'd learned penmanship from mimicking letters found on scrawled prescriptions from doctors, Rose's notes were artistic, the words flowing neatly and straight across the page. Maddux half expected to see lipstick smeared beneath the first time he read one of her messages because there appeared to be so much care taken with each pen stroke. But he soon learned she wrote everything that way.

Before reading the note, he inspected the shoes. The black leather wingtips had a set of instructions inserted inside, along with a diagram of how to operate the device. Rose also included a pair of sonic resistant earplugs, stored neatly in a small plastic bag.

Maddux returned his focus to the documents, removing the paperclip and sifting through the papers. It didn't take long before he confirmed his suspicions.

I know who Medved is.

XXVIII

MADDUX MADE A QUICK EXCUSE to his supervisor about why he needed to urgently go home and then hustled to the train station. Using his position at Opel as a cover, he didn't anticipate any problems getting back into Yugoslavia. All the trouble he could handle would be waiting for him once he arrived.

He checked his watch and noted that he had less than five minutes before the train's final boarding call. Rushing over to a payphone, he called Pritchett.

"Where are you?" Pritchett asked. "You sound like you're at the train station."

"I am," Maddux said. "I have some business to attend to."

"Hopefully not the kind of business I told you to avoid."

"Unfortunately, sir, this can't wait."

"You listen here, Maddux. You're going to get yourself killed if you keep acting so recklessly," Pritchett said with a growl. "I'm fine with letting you test your limits, but you're bordering on insanity right now, not to mention insubordination."

"I know what you're thinking—and this isn't about my father. This is about something else, something very important right now."

"I'm sure it is—but I'm also sure it can wait."

"You're not wrong often," Maddux said, "but you're wrong about this. I have to go, but I wanted to see if you could reach Dex in Belgrade."

"What on earth for?"

"He's in grave danger."

The whistle blew, signaling the final boarding call.

"What from?" Pritchett asked.

"I don't have time to explain now; just promise me that you'll warn him if you can reach him."

"Oh, Maddux, I swear you'll be the death of me one day."

"Promise?" Maddux said again.

He didn't wait to hear Pritchett's reply, instead hanging up hurriedly and racing toward the platform where the train was starting to chug down the track. Maddux jumped onto the bottom step leading into one of the passenger cars and lingered outside for a moment before taking his seat.

* * *

MADDUX AWOKE to the engineer's voice as the train clattered along the tracks just outside of Belgrade. The advance notification over the intercom that they were approaching Belgrade was news Maddux welcomed. His arms had grown sore from hugging his briefcase tight against his chest. Using a shoulder strap, he also carried a small overnight satchel, signifying Maddux's confidence that the trip would be short.

He shuffled through customs, opening his briefcase for the agent to demonstrate that he wasn't bringing any contraband into the country. Maddux had discovered the searches at the station were far less intrusive than those performed at the border, a fact he appreciated since he had a gun stashed inside his attaché case's secret compartment.

Once Maddux cleared customs, he hailed a cab and gave the man the address. The driver complained about all the traffic, even though rush hour had long gone. Maddux checked his watch. A few minutes past 9:00 p.m. Maddux had no idea if anyone would be there when he arrived, but he determined that whatever he found, he would be ready.

Maddux kept his head down as he entered the apartment complex, trying to remain as inconspicuous as possible. He nodded politely to an elderly woman carrying a poodle before stepping onto the elevator and ascending to the top floor, where Walt Kensington's apartment was located.

When Maddux stepped off the elevator, he noticed there were only two doors in the hallway. The door on the left was wide open as the unit was obviously undergoing some type of renovation. The one on the right was cracked by a few inches, and Maddux could hear voices coming from inside. He crouched low as he glanced up at the number on the door.

It was Kensington's apartment.

Maddux peered through the crack in an attempt to gauge the situation before entering the room. In the living room area, he could see several familiar faces along with one he'd never seen before. Dex and Kensington stood on one side, opposite of what looked like a KGB agent to Maddux. The man held a gun on Kensington. Between them stood the man Maddux was really after— Harvey Cordell.

When Maddux saw the report in the SDB prison in Konjic, he studied the handwriting. It looked familiar to him, as if he'd seen a report somewhere during his time in Germany written by the same person. After thinking through what he'd read in Konjic, his suspicion grew. The report hadn't been filled out by Kensington, who refused to write in cursive, a fact all too well known thanks to several outbursts over the demand that everyone use cursive by the CIA director once. But the script scrawled on Cordell's file was neat and efficient. And Maddux thought he'd seen it before. When Rose gave him the file, Maddux confirmed it was a match. Cordell had written the report for his own arrest by the KGB, which didn't seem right to Maddux. There were still plenty of questions to be answered, but the fact that Cordell had a gun trained on Dex told Maddux all he needed to know.

The men were arguing about something, mostly Kensington and Cordell going back and forth.

"Do you realize what you've done?" Kensington asked. "You're going to burn over half the assets in Eastern Europe."

Cordell wagged his finger at Kensington. "You think if I just gave them everything then they would let me live? Keeping secrets is how I stay alive; it's how I live."

"And revealing them is how you live, too—only you obviously aren't caring about the people whose lives you destroy."

Cordell used his left hand to deliver a sucker punch to Kensington's gut. After crumpling to the ground, Kensington absorbed several more blows to the stomach and face before blacking out.

The other agent in the room chuckled. "This is working out more perfectly than we thought. We will stage this like these men got into a shootout. And you'll be able to return to the CIA as a celebrated hero."

Maddux determined he couldn't wait any longer. He raced into the room, his gun trained on Cordell.

"I hate to put a kink in your plan, but that's not happening," Maddux said.

"Just when I thought this couldn't get any better, the Lone Ranger shows up," Cordell said with a grin. "You're gonna make this even easier than I thought because knowing you, you're defying orders and haven't told anyone your suspicions."

"Don't be so sure," Maddux said, glancing in the corner to see an unfamiliar man gagged and bound. "I have all my bases covered."

Cordell shook his head. "Except for the one behind you."

Maddux didn't move. "Why don't you drop your weapon, *Medved?*"

"Congratulations, you figured me out," Cordell said.

"There aren't any super assassins, are there?" Maddux asked.

"They're coming, but for now, I'll have to suffice," Cordell said before he nonchalantly redirected his gun toward Kensington and fired a shot, hitting him in the center of his forehead. Kensington was dead before he hit the floor.

Dex gasped while Maddux narrowed his eyes.

"If there's going to be another bullet fired in this room, there will be one put in your head," Maddux said.

"Maddux, just calm down and don't be so foolish," Cordell said. "It's not too late to join me. But if you continue to insist on fighting, things won't end well for you. In the end, you'd be on the wrong side of things—if you were alive."

"You're the one who isn't going to make it out of here alive tonight."

"Perhaps, but like I mentioned earlier, you still need to check your six."

Maddux refused to turn around.

With his gun still trained on Dex, Cordell shrugged. "Okay, my friend, don't say I didn't warn you."

Maddux winced as he felt a small blunt object shoved into his back.

"Weapon on the ground," a woman said.

Maddux knelt down slowly and placed his gun on the ground. He turned to see the elderly woman he had noticed in the lobby carrying a poodle.

"Over there," the woman snapped, directing him with her gun.

Crouching low, Maddux kept his hands in front of him.

"Keep those things where I can see them, or else I'll blow your head clean off," she said.

Maddux slid his hand along the side of his shoes, flicking a button that set off a horrific sonic sound. Everyone fell to the ground, clutched their ears, and begged for someone to make the noise stop.

Maddux worked quickly to strip Cordell, the woman, and the other KGB agent of their weapons before grouping them together in the corner. None of them even attempted to fight back due to the searing pain caused by the device. Once Maddux was satisfied he could manage the situation, he turned off the noise and handed Dex a weapon.

"While you're still wet behind the ears, Maddux, you do have impeccable timing," Dex said. "I have to give you that."

Maddux nodded as he took his earplugs out. "I do what I can. Now, why don't we go with Cordell's suggestion and make this look like a shootout? There's no way we're getting out of the country alive with him, nor am I leaving a KGB agent around as a witness. Besides, Cordell just murdered Kensington—and I think it's fair for us to act as judge and jury in this instance."

"I couldn't agree with you more."

"Who's the guy in the corner?" Maddux asked.

"That's Jovan Divac. He's a courier for us at the Belgrade station, but his cover is obviously blown. We need to get him and his family out of here."

"We'll get to you in a minute," Maddux said to Divac. "But before we do, I've got a couple of questions for Medved."

"Go to hell," Cordell snarled.

"So, just for curiosity's sake, what were you doing in the Konjic prison anyway?" Maddux asked. "Running an undercover op?"

"That old codger Pritchett wouldn't talk, so I convinced the KGB to let me get into the prison and get the information out of him," Cordell said.

Maddux crossed his arms. "But you saw us and knew we had to be planning an escape. Why didn't you warn them?"

"Nobody except Jankovic knew who I really was," Cordell said. "That's how it is, for better or worse. He was supposed to come see me that night, but apparently he got too drunk on all that wine you sold him and forgot."

"Most fortuitous for us, wouldn't you say?" Maddux asked with a grin.

"I'm done talking to you," Cordell said. "You won't always be so lucky, Maddux. Your end is coming sooner than you think."

"Maybe, but your time's up first, *Medved*."

Maddux didn't hesitate as he pulled the trigger.

XXIX

PRITCHETT WALKED INTO the conference room and threw a copy of the *Novosti* on the table. He surveyed all the agents in attendance along with Al Bearden. Each one had been instrumental in not only identifying and eliminating the mole but also in saving Pritchett's life.

"According to today's edition of the Belgrade paper, I'd say this was a successful mission," Pritchett said with a smile.

Maddux scooped up the *Novosti* and looked at the headline. "Care to translate that for us, Dex?"

"Four Dead in Shootout," Dex read aloud.

"We need to say a prayer for Kensington, God rest his soul," Pritchett said, making the sign of the cross. "He deserved a better fate. He was a devoted patriot and a good friend."

"What happens to the Belgrade station now?" Dex asked. "With Kensington gone and Cordell telling who knows what to the KGB and SDB, who can pick up the pieces there without getting burned again?"

Bearden shifted in his chair. "For now, we're going to channel everything back to our offices in London. All the agents on the ground will continue with their covers and will be contacted when we need them to be reactivated. We feel like it's critical for us to lay low for a while there when it comes to local leadership. Meanwhile, those assigned to listening posts will continue as usual and report any intelligence learned from captured conversations."

"Anything else we need to know about?" one of the agents asked.

"Based on Maddux's and Dex's report, it sounds like the KGB super assassin story is a myth," Pritchett said. "Gentlemen, either of you care to elaborate?"

Dex nodded at Maddux.

"Cordell admitted that there were no KGB super assassins, though he did suggest that it wasn't entirely made up," Maddux said. "The truth is all of our agents who were captured or killed recently were done so as a direct result of the intel Cordell gave them. It's not that the KGB agents possessed some incredible skills as much as they knew everything about our people."

"So, we can expect KGB super assassins to surface in the future?" Pritchett asked.

Maddux shrugged. "Maybe, or maybe Cordell was just trying to say something to throw us off, a last-ditch effort to lash out at us. I don't think we need to cower in fear at the possibility that there are some KGB agents with special training to track and kill our people, but I also don't think we need to dismiss it outright."

"We're connecting with our contacts within the KGB to learn more," Bearden said. "But for now, we just don't know. Of course, the KGB is always trying to mitigate our ability to do our job, but to what extent this rumor is true remains a mystery. Rest assured I will pass along more information as it becomes available."

"Any other questions for now?" Pritchett asked.

The room remained silent.

"In that case, I want to take this opportunity to thank all of you for the role you played in retrieving me from the Konjic prison. I know Maddux and Dex—and even Rose—all took personal risks to get me out of there. And for your efforts, I am extremely grateful. To be honest, I think they were ready to get me out of there. Not many people want anything to do with a one-eyed man walking around with a hook. There's no telling how long I would've been there—if they decided to let me live—had you not rescued me."

"I can speak for all of us in saying that we're glad you're back," Bearden said. "You run a great station here in Bonn, and I quickly found out just how loyal everyone here is to you."

"The real challenge is keeping it that way," Pritchett said with a chuckle. "But I'd take anyone in this room over anyone else in the agency."

Bearden stood. "Well, it looks like my work here is done. I've got a little paperwork to sign before I leave and return to London. But I'll do so knowing this station is back in good hands."

"Thank you, sir," Pritchett said before turning his gaze to the rest of the attendees. "The rest of you can get back to work as well, except for you, Maddux. We need to talk."

Pritchett watched the rest of the agents file out of

the room until he was left alone with Maddux.

"I wanted to thank you privately for what you did," Pritchett said. "It was stupid for you to call Rose and ask her to come help you, especially without telling her all the facts about your situation, but it worked out. Just don't do it again."

"Understood," Maddux said.

"But that's not all," Pritchett said. "I have a special mission for you that I want you to run."

"Is it dangerous? Because I'd like to request a small break from nearly getting killed."

Pritchett smiled. "No, this one is simple. Just a recruiting mission."

"What do I have to do?"

"Convince Gunnar Andersson to help the CIA."

"I thought you said it was simple."

XXX

A DAY BEFORE the French Grand Prix, Maddux entered the race garage in search of Gunnar Andersson. Maddux found the assignment intriguing, even though he had never recruited anyone before. His own recruitment process in New York was one based out of desperation, far from the textbook way taught during his training. The method was simplistic—explain the need, sell the vision, share the benefits, close the deal. Delivering the end result the agency wanted was the real challenge.

Maddux dodged forklifts zipping around the area transporting tires to different race teams. Power tools buzzed and mechanics yelled out instructions, sounds that could only be heard in between the intermittent revving of a car engine. When Maddux found Andersson's designated spot, two mechanics were working beneath the car. Maddux knocked on the door and waited.

One of the mechanics slid out from beneath the car. "If you're looking for Andersson, you won't find him here."

"Do you know where I can find him?"

"Try the track. He always walks it a day before the race."

The Charade track was new to Formula 1, having only hosted motorcycle races. And since Andersson had never raced anything but cars, Maddux realized every straightaway and turn at Charade would be foreign to Andersson.

"Thanks for the tip," Maddux said as he headed for his car.

Maddux turned onto the course and drove slowly, searching for Andersson and finally catching up with him at the Courbes de Manson, one of the track's famed curves.

"Need a lift?" Maddux asked after pulling up next to Andersson.

Andersson waved him off, refusing to even look inside the car. "It's the day before the race. I always walk the course."

"I promise this will be nothing like Barcelona," Maddux said.

Andersson abruptly halted and stooped down to peer through the open driver's side window. "I thought I recognized your voice. And I most definitely will not be getting in a car with you."

Andersson resumed his walk. Maddux gunned his car and shot ahead of Andersson, parking along the shoulder of the road. Leaning against his car, Maddux pulled out a Lucky Strike and waited for Andersson to catch up.

"Those things will kill you," Andersson said as he reached Maddux, who joined the driver.

"So will working for the CIA, but neither one of those things scare me that much. And quite frankly, they're probably both safer than strapping yourself into a box surrounded by gasoline and hurtling over a hundred miles an hour around hairpin turns."

Andersson flashed a wry grin. "That's why I smoke, too. Why deny myself one of life's simple pleasures when I'm going to die soon anyway?"

"I like your style," Maddux said. "That's why I'm here to talk with you today and see if you're interested in a unique opportunity."

Andersson stopped, furrowed his brow, and gave Maddux a sideways glance. "After what happened in Barcelona, you expect me to trust you again?"

"You know that was a misunderstanding."

"A *big* misunderstanding, so big that it's hard believe you didn't understand what you were doing. You thought I was an assassin for the KGB? It's so ridiculous that I don't even know how to respond to it."

"I may have something that sounds even more ridiculous, if you want to hear it."

Andersson sighed. "Humor me."

"We want you to work for the CIA."

Andersson broke into laughter as he resumed walking. "You want me to work with you? That might be the funniest thing I've heard in a long time."

Maddux hustled to catch up. "Look, if you don't want to help us, I understand. Our relationship got off on the wrong foot."

"You call this a relationship? It feels more like you are a crazy stalker, someone who just can't accept the fact that there never was a relationship, much less that there was one to repair in the first place."

"You're right," Maddux said. "Things were bad, but there is an explanation. We had an agent who used you to deflect us away from what he was doing."

"And what happened to this agent?"

"I killed him," Maddux said coldly.

"You what?"

"You heard me. I killed him."

"Are you going to kill me too if I don't join your CIA?"

Maddux shook his head. "If you decide this isn't something you want to do, feel free to walk away knowing that we'll never contact you again."

"After you shoot me?"

"That's not how we do things," Maddux said. "What's the point in having to coerce someone to work for you? At some point when their interests are better suited to go in another direction, they will burn you. But if you choose to do this on your own, then you'll have a lifetime partnership—or at least one that won't vanish when the person decides to move on."

"Let's suppose for a moment that I want to help you. Tell me why I would do it."

"You're an honest man who wants to make a difference in the world and realize that simply driving a fast car around a track many times is never going to help you make an impact. You'll just always be a guy who sped around a racetrack."

"And what would you want me to do?"

"Nothing too dangerous," Maddux said. "Plant a few bugs here and there. Pass intelligence to us from another agent. Keep an eye on the KGB. You have unfettered access to places we can't get close to."

Andersson stroked his chin and stopped walking. "This all sounds rather interesting. What's in it for me?"

"You'll be handsomely compensated for your participation. I may even be able to work in an appearance for an Opel commercial."

"That sounds interesting. Let me mull it over and get back with you."

Maddux pulled out a business card and scribbled a number on the back. "This is where you can reach me while I'm in town. You have until the end of the day to make your decision. After that, my offer expires."

Andersson nodded and continued walking.

"I'll be awaiting your decision," Maddux called before he spun and walked in the other direction.

XXXI

THREE DAYS LATER, Maddux settled onto a bench near a sidewalk that ran along the Rhine River. The peaceful easy flowing water soothed his mind when he was troubled. Despite the way his position with the CIA gave him a renewed sense of purpose, Maddux felt a deep disappointment. The point of agreeing to work with the CIA was to uncover the mystery behind his father's disappearance. But so far, Maddux had found nothing but dead ends or well-constructed roadblocks

"Is this seat taken?" a woman asked.

Maddux looked up to see Rose standing in front of him. His gaze lingered on her face for a moment before he answered her. Rose's hair whipped around her face in the gentle breeze. She tucked her locks behind her ears, her arched eyebrows pleading for an answer.

"Of course not," Maddux finally said. "It's all for you."

She sat next to him and took his hands in hers. "What's wrong, Ed? You haven't seemed yourself since you got back from France. Did something happen there?"

Maddux shook his head. "Just something I've been thinking about."

"Care to share?"

He shrugged and turned his gaze to the Rhine. "Things haven't worked out like I'd hoped."

Rose released his hands. "Regarding what?"

"The real reason why I joined the CIA—to find out about what happened to my father."

"That's actually what I wanted to talk with you about. It's why I'm here."

"What is it this time?"

Rose smoothed out her skirt and cleared her throat. "I don't really know how to tell you this, especially if you're already dealing with disappointment about how information about your father has been kept secret from you. So, I'm just going to say it."

"Out with it then."

"That house you went to in Barcelona, the one you found an address for in Kensington's office."

"Yeah, I remember."

"Well, turns out we have someone listening to every communication that goes in and out of that house. And the day you went, someone made a call right after you left."

"And?"

"Apparently, whoever lives there knew exactly what you were talking about and called someone else to tell them that you were looking for your father."

"But you don't know who they called?"

She shook her head.

"So, who's house was I at?" he asked.

"That's where things get really interesting. It's a former CIA station chief, Gil Williams."

"What station?"

"Moscow."

Maddux shook his head. "I'm not sure what to think about this."

"Well, your father obviously had some connection to Williams."

"And Williams has some vested interest in making sure I don't speak with him."

Rose scooted forward to the edge of the bench and turned more toward Maddux. "Look, I know this isn't great news necessarily, but I'm telling you this as a warning—and as your friend—because you need to be careful. Why the CIA doesn't want you to know about your father is the million-dollar question right now, but we're going to get to the bottom of it eventually. But just try not to force the issue, okay? I don't want something terrible to happen to you."

"What does that mean?" Maddux asked as he furrowed his brow. "It almost sounds like you're—"

"I just mean that I'm concerned about you, that's all."

"You are on my side, right? I need to know that you're with me, no matter what the agency directs you to do."

Rose exhaled slowly. "I'll do whatever I can to help you."

"That's not what I asked. I need to know that you're with me."

She nodded. "This isn't easy for me to go up against the organization that I love and am passionate about. I may be naïve, but I tend to think we do good work here, the kind of work that keeps people safe and evil at bay."

"If it were only that simple," Maddux said. "Make no mistake about the fact that I'm a patriot, but I see far more shades of grey in this world than I do black and white. But right now, I'm seeing nothing but darkness from the agency when it comes to my father."

"We'll figure this out together, don't worry," she said. "I am on your side, Ed. Always."

She leaned over and gave him a kiss on the cheek before getting up and shuffling away.

Maddux buried his head in his hands as he remained on the bench. He wanted to revel in the fact that Rose had just kissed him, but he couldn't think about anything other than the appearance of a conspiracy within the CIA to keep him from learning the truth about his father. After a few minutes, his silence was interrupted by Pritchett.

"Nothing beats the Rhine twinkling under the street lamps and night sky," Pritchett said. "Though it's difficult to see when you're looking down."

Maddux looked up at his boss. "I'm having a difficult time seeing much beauty in the world these days."

"Well, that's your own fault," Pritchett said. "You've got a smart and attractive woman who has the hots for you. You have a job that sends you all over the world to exotic locations. You just snuffed out a mole in the CIA. And your first recruiting mission was a success with Gunnar Andersson. What in the world is keeping you from enjoying the moment and seeing your fantastic life for what it is?"

"My father—I still don't really know much more about him, despite promises to get more information about him and what happened to him."

Pritchett sat on the bench next to Maddux. "It's a complicated world we live in. And to be honest, if I knew more, I'd tell you. But I can't because I don't know any more than you do at this point, nor do I have access to any of the files that might tell us what really happened."

"So, this was a bait and switch with me? Try to lure me in by dangling the carrot of my father in front of me but then hope I'd just get hooked on wanting to help my country?"

"I swear that was never the plan," Pritchett said. "I like to be forthright in all my recruitments. And I intend to keep my word and find out as much as I can for you. But right now, you can't dwell on that. You just have to do what needs to be done, and the rest will fall into place."

"I've heard that before, and it's a worn out line."

"Look at me," Pritchett said as he put his hand on Maddux's shoulder.

Maddux turned to face the station chief.

"I am on your side," Pritchett said. "Our agency's greatest asset is people. And I've never lost sight of that. If you need help, I will help you, but it might just take more time than you would like. Understand?"

Maddux nodded.

"Now, with that said, I'm still not going to discourage you from looking," Pritchett said. "Rose told me about the phone call Gil Williams placed, so when you come to the office in the morning, I'll give you everything we have on him. You can look through it and see if you can find something that makes the connection for you regarding your father."

"Do you know Gil?"

"I've crossed paths with him in the past, but it's been a while. He never struck me as someone who would sell out, but he was given an early retirement rather abruptly—and not of his own volition, from what I understand."

"That sounds rather suspicious."

Pritchett patted Maddux on his knee. "I'll let you draw your own conclusions after you sift through all the papers. In the meantime, I've got a new assignment for you regarding a new recruit. You did such a good job convincing Andersson to join that I thought I'd let you try your hand again. But this time, I want you to oversee an entire recruiting program."

"And what is this program going to do?"

"I'll tell you in the morning. Have a good night— and don't forget to admire the Rhine before you go home."

Maddux nodded knowingly at Pritchett, who appeared to wink. Maddux wasn't sure since Pritchett's right eye was covered with a patch, but it sure seemed like that's what happened.

Exhaling slowly, Maddux took Pritchett's advice and stared out at the river.

Gil Williams. Just who exactly are you, and why don't you want me to learn anything else about my father?

Maddux's spirit lifted as he stood and began his walk home.

ACKNOWLEDGMENTS

Starting a new series is always frightening territory for an author. Until readers start tearing into a story, I always wonder if they are going to resonate with my characters and with the storyline. So far, the feedback I've received on the first book in the Ed Maddux series has been encouraging, and I hope that continues as the series progresses.

The bulk of my research for this novel took place at the National Archives, and I'm incredibly grateful to Steven Hamilton for his direction there. Finding these CIA papers from the 1960s wasn't easy, and I doubt I would've ever thought to look for them had it not been for him.

As usual, I appreciate the editing skills of Krystal Wade in making sure this book is fit for publication.

And as always, I must thank my wife for listening to me babble on about espionage while I worked away on crafting this story.

Last but not least, I want to thank you, the reader, for supporting my work. I hope you enjoyed reading this book as much as I enjoyed writing it.

ABOUT THE AUTHOR

R.J. PATTERSON is an award-winning writer living in the Pacific Northwest. He first began his illustrious writing career as a sports journalist, recording his exploits on the soccer fields in England as a young boy. Then when his father told him that people would pay him to watch sports if he would write about what he saw, he went all in. He landed his first writing job at age 15 as a sports writer for a daily newspaper in Orangeburg, S.C. He later attended earned a degree in newspaper journalism from the University of Georgia, where he took a job covering high school sports for the award-winning *Athens Banner-Herald* and *Daily News*.

He later became the sports editor of *The Valdosta Daily Times* before working in the magazine world as an editor and freelance journalist. He has won numerous writing awards, including a national award for his investigative reporting on a sordid tale surrounding an NCAA investigation over the University of Georgia football program.

R.J. enjoys the great outdoors of the Northwest while living there with his wife and four children. He still follows sports closely and enjoys coaching his daughter's soccer team.

He also loves connecting with readers and would love to hear from you. To stay updated about future projects, connect with him over Facebook, on Twitter or Instagram (@MrRJPatterson) or on the interwebs at:

www.RJPbooks.com